These girls are on the adventure of their and their own special abilities, they just newest heroes . . .

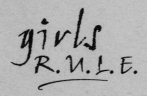

Kayla Adams's wavy brown hair and dark, almond-shaped eyes attract attention, but her quick temper and sharp tongue keep it—especially when she stands up for her friends.

Carson McDonald has never let her hearing disability get in her way. In fact, it has forced this blonde, beautiful athlete to be extra-sensitive to her environment—qualities which make her an excellent sleuth.

Becca Fisher is a natural clown, always cracking jokes. But her sarcastic sense of humor often has a way of getting the petite, wiry girl with deep green eyes in trouble.

Sophie Schultz is intense, determined, and stubborn. Nicknamed "little bulldog" by her dad, this redhead knows what she wants and goes after it despite all obstacles, including her older brother and junior ranger, Kyle!

Alex Loomis-Drake has a million facts stored in her head, and a million interests to match. But although this girl with brown, silky hair comes from a wealthy family, she isn't your usual pampered princess.

Don't miss any of the girls R. U. L. E. *adventures!*

girls R.U.L.E.

#1

GIRLS TO THE RESCUE

Kris Lowe

BERKLEY JAM BOOKS, NEW YORK

To Fiona, who rules.

GIRLS R.U.L.E.: GIRLS TO THE RESCUE

A Berkley Jam Book / published by arrangement with the author

PRINTING HISTORY
Berkley Jam edition / October 1998

The Penguin Putnam Inc. World Wide Web site address is http://www.penguinputnam.com

ISBN: 0-425-16609-0

BERKLEY JAM BOOKS®
Berkley Jam Books are published by The Berkley Publishing Group, a member of Penguin Putnam Inc., 200 Madison Avenue, New York, New York 10016.
BERKLEY JAM and its logo are trademarks belonging to Berkley Publishing Corporation.

PRINTED IN THE UNITED STATES OF AMERICA

10 9 8 7 6 5 4 3 2 1

SOPHIE

ONE

I knew something was up as soon as I saw my mother standing in the doorway to my room with her hands on her hips.

I was sitting on my rag rug, still dressed in the tie-dyed tank top and patched jeans I'd worn to school, and I was painting each of my toenails a different color. I never polish my fingernails—I think it looks tacky—but I love to make rainbow toenails. My golden retriever, Lemonade, was lying nearby, and my new CD, *Reckless Goulash* by the Strawberries, was playing on the stereo. I'm totally into new bands and alternative music. I probably have one of the biggest CD collections in the whole freshman class of Cayenga High School.

Anyway, there was no doubt about it. My mother definitely had *that look* on her face. I knew I was in big trouble.

"Hi, Mom," I said, trying to sound cheerful.

She sighed. "Sophie." She crossed my room and turned

down my music. Then she shook her head. "I don't know what I have to do to get you and your brother to do your part around here. I leave you notes, but you don't pay any attention to them. I can't do everything, you know."

My mom can be pretty tough sometimes. She's a great mom, and she loves me and my brother Jason a lot and everything. But she gets worked up about certain things. Especially when she's tired, which is a lot of the time. I guess it's partly from having to work all the time and raise us on her own. I've tried to remember how she was before, when my dad still lived with us, but it's hard. I was only seven when he left. Now he lives back east, in Pennsylvania, and I don't see him very much.

I waited. This was my least favorite way of getting in trouble. I hate having to guess what it is that I did.

My mother sighed again. "Sophie? The newspapers? Tomorrow's recycling day, remember? You and Jason were supposed to bundle them this afternoon before I got home from work."

I cringed. "Mom, I'm sorry. I *meant* to do it."

"Well, you can do it now," she said firmly.

"What about Jason?" I asked. "He has to help, right?"

"Jason's not here," my mother replied.

Now it was my turn to sigh. "Figures," I mumbled.

My brother must have some of kind of anti-chore radar or something. Whenever there's work to be done, he's suddenly practically on the other side of the world.

"He went over to Rick's," my mother said. "But he'll help you as soon as he gets back."

Yeah, sure, whenever that is, I added silently.

I stood up and slipped my feet, with their still-wet nails, into my leather thong sandals. I headed out of the room and down the stairs, with Lemonade close behind me.

I opened the kitchen door and stepped into the garage. Lemonade slipped by me and out of the garage into the warm California evening air. Wagging her tail happily, she ran across the lawn. Well, it's not exactly a lawn. It's more like a small square of grass in front of my family's house. Anyway, Lemonade was across it and under the bushes toward the Frankels' place next door in no time.

"Lemonade!" I called. "Remember, no digging up Mrs. Frankel's flowers!" I sighed. *Like she's really going to listen to me,* I added silently.

I tied my long, curly red hair into a quick knot at the base of my head and started bundling the newspapers, tying them with twine. There was no sign of Jason—of course. Finally, after I'd finished bundling at least half of the papers on my own, I saw him headed up the driveway with his friend Rick Neely.

Oh, great, I said to myself, sighing.

I'm sorry, but I just can't stand Rick Neely. Not that I'm the kind of person who doesn't get along with people or anything like that. In fact, usually I'm just the opposite. But there's something about Rick that really irritates me. Maybe it's because he acts like such a big shot, like he's an expert on everything. And you can tell he thinks he's really handsome, too, with his jet-black hair and green eyes. Trouble is, a lot of the girls at Cayenga High agree with him.

Jason and Rick were tossing a basketball back and forth, laughing. They didn't give me a second look, but headed straight for the door that led into the kitchen.

"Jason!" I called as I heard the door bang behind them.

There was no answer, only more laughter from inside the house. I headed into the kitchen after them.

"Jason," I said again.

"What, Soppy?" Jason replied, heading for the refrigerator. He took out some milk and started swigging it straight from the carton.

"Jason, that's gross," I said. "Use a glass. And don't call me that."

Referring to me as "Soppy" is Jason's idea of humor. He thinks it's hysterically funny that when I was around two or something I had trouble saying "Sophie" so I used to pronounce it "Soppy." Not that Jason can actually remember that. After all, he's only a year older than I am. I'm sure he just saw it on one of our family videos. But he's definitely not about to let me forget it. That's the kind of brother Jason is.

Rick started bouncing the basketball on the kitchen floor.

"Hey Jason, think fast!" Rick lobbed the ball at my brother, who almost dropped the carton of milk as he went to catch it. Jason laughed as he threw the ball back.

"Watch out!" I cried as the ball whizzed by my head.

"Watch out!" Rick mimicked. He laughed and threw the ball back. "Why do girls have to be such wimps?"

That's exactly the kind of Rick comment I can't stand. And of course my brother laughed at it. Sometimes I think Rick has some kind of mysterious power over Jason. If Rick thinks something's funny, Jason thinks it's funny. If Rick thinks something's cool, Jason thinks it's cool. Maybe it's because Rick is sixteen, a year older than Jason. Rick's on the varsity basketball team, and Jason only made the JV team this year. Rick's also the unofficial captain of the junior rangers at Cayenga Park. Cayenga Park is this huge national park right at the edge of our town. It goes all the way from the mountains east of Cayenga down to the Pacific coast. There are canyons and a vineyard, and people camp and rock-climb there. Jason joined the junior rangers this year, too, probably because Rick told him it was cool. Anyway, now Jason likes to tromp around the park acting like a big shot with Rick and the other junior rangers.

"Very funny," I said to Rick. "We'll see how funny it is when Mom comes downstairs and finds out you guys are playing ball in the kitchen, Jason."

Rick was still snickering, but I noticed that Jason put the basketball down on a chair. I guess when it comes down to it even Rick's mysterious power over Jason still isn't much of a match for my mom's power.

"We're supposed to do the newspapers," I continued. "Recycling tomorrow. Mom's pretty mad that we forgot."

"Hey, Jason, I thought we were going to shoot some hoops in your driveway," Rick said.

Jason stuck the milk back in the refrigerator. "I guess I better not, Rick. Maybe some other time."

Rick shrugged, a smirk on his face. "Suit yourself, man. See you tomorrow in school."

Rick took his basketball and left, and Jason followed me into the garage.

"You sure took your time getting home," I commented to him. "I've already done a ton of work by myself."

"So it's almost all finished?" Jason asked, looking hopefully around the garage.

"Nice try," I replied. "There's a bunch more over in the corner. And *you* can do them."

"All of them? No way!" he objected.

"This is my last one." I pulled a piece of string tight around the bundle of papers I'd gathered. But as I was about to tie it, something caught my eye.

"Hey, look at this," I said.

"What?" Jason asked, glancing up from his papers.

"They're starting a girls' division of the junior rangers," I told him.

"Oh, that." Jason knotted some twine and broke it off in his fingers.

"You knew about it already?" I asked Jason. "How come you didn't say anything?"

Jason shrugged. "What's to say?" He laughed. "It's not like *you're* about to join, Soppy."

Now that made me mad. "What makes you so sure?" I shot back.

"Oh, come on," Jason said. "You have to be in top shape to be a ranger."

"*Junior* ranger," I corrected.

"Whatever," Jason said. "Either way, you have to admit you're not exactly the athletic type. You've never even gone out for a team in your life."

I didn't say anything. Jason was right. I'm definitely not the muscle-girl type. My mom says I'm probably going to be curvy, like her, when I grow up. Which is okay with me, I guess. But still, I didn't like Jason's attitude.

Jason grinned. "Besides, Rick says no girl is ever going to make it through the tryouts anyway."

"Rick is such a lame-brain," I said. "I'm sure lots of girls will make it."

Jason shook his head. "Rick says the qualifying test is way too tough for girls. A lot of *guys* don't even make it, you know. Anyway, the last thing the rangers need is a bunch of girls running around the park getting in their way."

"I can't believe you just said that!" I sputtered, furious now. "Besides, aren't you forgetting that the park already has women rangers, too? I think it's totally unfair that there's been a boys' junior division all these years but no girls' division."

"You don't have to get all worked up about it, Soppy," Jason replied. "Anyway, girls aren't into stuff like that. I bet nobody even shows up to try out."

"What makes you so sure?" I said. "I bet lots of girls will try out. I bet lots will make it, too. And they'll probably end up being better junior rangers than you guys."

Jason laughed. "Oh, yeah, right!" he said sarcastically.

I could feel my face burning. "Jason, you are turning into as much of a lame-brain as Rick Neely!" I shot out.

Now Jason looked mad. "Why don't you just be quiet about Rick, Sophie!"

Cayenga Echo

OCTOBER 2, 1998　　VOLUME 20, NO. 8　　CAYENGA, CALIFORNIA

SECTION 2—ARTS & ENTERTAINMENT

JUNIOR PARK RANGERS WILL ADD GIRLS' DIVISION

Parks supervisor says move is "long overdue"

OCTOBER 1: Lydia Rodriguez, the newly appointed regional parks supervisor for the Cayenga Park area, announced today that she plans to create a new girls' division of the park's Ranger Unit Learning Extension.

The current Extension, known locally as the "junior rangers," was developed ten years ago to assist the Park Ranger Unit in its management of Cayenga Park. Until now, the junior rangers' group has been open to young men between the ages of 13 and 17. The new division will be open to young women of the same age.

Ms. Rodriguez, a former park ranger herself, says that the creation of the girls extension is something that is long overdue. Asked how she plans to find the funds for the new extension in a parks department budget that is already stretched to the limit, Ms. Rodriguez replied that she will be looking at other, "nonessential" Cayenga Park programs to see if cuts can be made.

Young men wishing to join the Extension have traditionally been required to pass a difficult physical test and to prove their knowledge of the park. Ms. Rodriguez and Ranger Abe Mayfield of the park say that the girls will have to pass the same exam in order to work with the rangers. All girls of qualifying age who are interested are invited to take the test at the Park Headquarters on Saturday, October 13 at 10:00 A.M.

Supervisor Rodriguez says she hopes the addition of the girls' unit will

(continued on page 14)

LOCAL REACTION:
Is the new division of the rangers' extension a good idea?
—see page 5

"You be quiet!" I yelled back.

"You don't even know what you're talking about!" my brother said angrily. "Rick's right. You don't know the first thing about the junior rangers. And if you think there are really going to be girls working in the park you must be dreaming!"

I glared at him and clenched my teeth. "We'll see who's dreaming. . . ."

"Oh, yeah? What are you going to do, try out yourself?" Jason's voice was mocking.

I folded my arms across my chest. "Maybe I am."

Jason laughed. "What a joke. You know you don't mean it."

"I *do* mean it," I insisted. "I *am* trying out for the girls' division, Jason, and no one—not you, not lame-brain Rick—*no one* can stop me!"

TWO

Oh my gosh, what did I do this time?

That was all I could think as I lay in bed later that night. Everyone else was asleep, including Lemonade, who was curled up on the braided rug by my bed. But I lay in bed staring at my ceiling, feeling kind of sick.

What made me think I could try out for the rangers? I can barely make it up the rope in gym class. Me and my big mouth. I turned over in bed and let out a groan.

I hadn't *meant* to tell Jason that I wanted to try out for the girls' junior rangers. It had just kind of popped out while we were arguing. And now that it had there was no way I could back down. For one thing, Jason would never let me forget it. I'd practically be sending Jason an invitation to tease me about it for the rest of my life.

And there was another thing, too. Once I set out to do something I don't usually turn back. Like when I was six and I wanted the training wheels off my bike. I guess I'd seen Jason and some of the bigger kids in the neighborhood riding that way, and I wanted to, too. I felt pretty nervous as I watched my dad take them off. I remember he stopped and asked me if I was sure I was ready. I was anything but ready—my insides felt like a washing machine on the spin cycle—but I wasn't about to back down.

I remember I spent the whole day trying to learn how to ride that bike, going up and down the driveway of the house we lived in back then. Every time I tried, I fell. My dad wanted to help me, but I was determined to do it on my own. Finally, just as the air was starting to cool, and my mom called me in for dinner, I got it. I was so excited, I started screaming. My knees and elbows were completely scraped up from falling so many times. But I didn't even care. All that mattered was that I had done it on my own.

That's the kind of stuff that made my dad come up with his nickname for me. I know it sounds kind of funny, but he's always called me "little bulldog." My dad says I'm like a bulldog because once I get my teeth into something nothing can make me let go. I guess that's what my mom means when she says I'm stubborn.

Still, I knew that telling Jason I was going to try out for the rangers might end up being one of the worst mistakes I'd ever made. I bit my lip, remembering what Jason had said about the test and how hard it was. I knew it couldn't be true that no girl could make it, like Rick had said. But that didn't necessarily mean that *I* could make it, either.

How hard could the test be? I wondered. Jason had taken it over the summer, and had been working in the park ever since. Jason wasn't the best athlete in the world.

But I wasn't an athlete at all!

I knew I couldn't ask Jason about it. He'd never tell me anything if he thought it might help me pass. Just thinking about all this was tying my stomach in knots. *What if I make a total fool out of myself?* I thought.

Finally, I sat up in bed and turned on the light. *Maybe I should go find the rest of that article in the paper. Maybe there will be something more in there about the test. Something that will help me, somehow.*

I swung my feet over the edge of my bed, and Lemonade opened one sleepy eye to look at me.

"Come on, girl," I whispered, standing up. I knew I'd feel a lot better going out to the newspapers in the dark if I had Lemonade by my side.

She stood up and followed me out of my room. We made our way through the dark house to the kitchen, and I pulled open the door.

I shivered a little in my nightshirt as I walked barefoot across the grass and down the driveway.

The newspapers were stacked where Jason and I had left them, by the garbage pails at the end of the driveway. Lemonade panted happily and wagged her tail. She began sniffing the hedges that led to Mrs. Frankel's house next door.

"Lemonade, stay!" I whispered.

She glanced at me and continued sniffing.

Quickly, I searched through the newspapers. I found the stack with the page I had seen earlier on top. *Hopefully the rest of the article is in this same pile,* I thought, picking up the bundle.

I called to Lemonade. But she was burrowing under the bushes. Finally, I put down the newspapers and got down on my hands and knees. I reached under the hedge and grabbed hold of her collar. Picking up the bundle of papers again with my free hand, I dragged Lemonade back to the house.

Back in my room, I picked up the first page of the newspaper and lay down on my stomach to look at it. As I reread the beginning of the article, I scanned it for details I might have missed the first time. I definitely liked the part where the new parks supervisor said that the girls' division was "long overdue." It was funny—I'd known about the junior rangers ever since I was little, but I had never wondered why there wasn't a girls' division. Now that I thought about it, though, it seemed totally unfair.

I continued reading until I came to the part about the qualifying test. But all the article said was that there was a difficult physical test and that you had to prove your knowledge of the park.

The article was supposed to be continued on page fourteen. I searched through the pile of papers. But they were all out of order. Page fourteen was nowhere to be found.

For a moment I considered going back out to the driveway. But page fourteen could be anywhere out there. It seemed crazy to try to go through all those other stacks of newspapers looking for it.

Something else did catch my eye, though, on page five. It was an interview feature. And there was Rick Neely's name, right in front of me!

I started reading.

QUESTION OF THE DAY: Newly appointed Regional Parks Supervisor Lydia Rodriquez has just announced plans to create a new girls' division of Cayenga Park's Ranger Unit Learning Extension. What do you think of the idea of girls as junior rangers?

RICK NEELY, age 16
Senior member, boys' unit, Learning Extension
"It'll never work. This is a hard job, and girls just aren't up to it. Besides, they have their own clubs at school, like cheerleading. I think we should keep the junior rangers just for boys."

ROBIN ALLERTON, age 29
Park ranger
"I think it's a great idea. The Learning Extension is a super training ground for actually becoming a ranger. I wish it had been around when I was a girl!"

DR. LYLE BURR, age 66
Wildlife researcher, Cayenga Park
"I don't think that any girls will want to join. I'm sure the park will soon realize that the program is unnecessary."

ABE MAYFIELD, age 52
Head, Ranger Unit
"I'm very happy to have more young people helping out in the park, girls or boys. I welcome the new unit."

CARSON MCDONALD, age 15
Aspiring member of new girls' division
"I'm trying out, for sure. My mom's a ranger, and I think it would be really fun to work in the park."

Reading Rick's words made me angry all over again. *How typical of Rick to think that all girls want to be cheerleaders!* I thought. Then I laughed. *I probably have less of a chance of ever becoming a cheerleader than I do of becoming a junior ranger,* I realized. Not that I'd want to. The cheerleaders at my school are all these perfect-looking petite girls with sleek ponytails, and they dress pretty preppy. They're all friends with each other, and they all go out with guys on the football team. I'm definitely not the cheerleading type.

I wasn't surprised to see that Carson McDonald was trying out for the junior rangers. Carson's a sophomore at Cayenga High, and she's kind of like a superjock. I didn't really know her, but she was in my ceramics class. Actually, the funny thing about Carson is that she sort of looks like she could be a cheerleader. She's really pretty, and she has shoulder-length, blonde hair, and she's in great shape. But although I didn't know her, she definitely didn't seem like the type who would want to stand on the sidelines and cheer. In fact, she was captain of a bunch of the girls' athletic teams. It seemed as though Carson wouldn't have too much trouble making the junior rangers.

What about me, though? I thought worriedly. *What if all the other girls who try out are jocks like Carson? Maybe I should just give up this whole idea after all.*

Then Rick Neely's name caught my eye again. I pictured his smirking face. *I can't let Rick get away with this,* I decided. *I can't back down. I have to show Rick—and Jason, too—that girls can be junior rangers. That I can be one. I have to go to those tryouts. I have to give it everything I've got, and I have to pass that test!*

THREE

The next morning, I met my friend Miranda Ruiz by our lockers at school. As usual, Miranda was there early and had everything organized for her day. She's the type who arrives ahead of time and has all her pencils sharpened and in a cute little pencil case. But I'm so rushed leaving my house that half the time I have to eat breakfast in my mom's car or on the school bus. I figure it's been a successful morning if I actually make it to school before the final bell without forgetting something major, like my backpack. Pencils and pens I consider to be extras.

"Hi, Sophie," Miranda said. "Do you want to go to the mall with me today after school? I've got some money I made baby-sitting and I want to get a new shirt."

I stopped twirling the lock on my locker for a moment. "I don't think so," I said, without looking up. "Thanks anyway, though."

"You sure?" Miranda pressed. "We could stop in at Tune Up and see if they got any new CDs in stock."

I knew she was trying to tempt me. But I shook my head. "I have to run."

"Why? Where are you rushing off to?" Miranda asked.

"No, I mean I actually have to *run,*" I corrected her. "Um, you know, as in jog?"

She stared at me. "Since when do you jog, Sophie?"

"Actually, since I decided to try out for the new division of the junior rangers," I said, trying to make my voice sound casual.

Miranda's eyes widened. "Are you kidding me?"

"No, but I kind of wish I was," I admitted. Then the whole story came pouring out. I told Miranda about the newspaper article, the argument with Jason, and the way I'd blurted out to him that I was going to take the ranger test.

Miranda looked sympathetic. "Sophie, you don't have to do this just because you had a fight with Jason," she said gently. "Besides, think about it. If you pass the test you'll have to be a junior ranger and work in the park and stuff. That's a pretty big thing to end up doing just because your brother said some dumb stuff to you."

"Believe me, *passing* the test is the last thing I have to worry about. I'm definitely more concerned with what will happen when I *don't* pass it," I told her. Still, Miranda had a point. I'd been so busy worrying about the test I hadn't thought about the fact that if I *did* pass they'd actually expect me to *be* a junior ranger.

I knew that the junior rangers helped the regular rangers with all their park duties, from patrolling the park to lifeguarding the beach at the cove to leading hiking groups up the trails—all stuff I just couldn't imagine myself doing, somehow. *On the other hand,* I thought, *I do love being outside, and Cayenga Park is really nice. Still,* me, *a junior ranger?* I just didn't know.

I shrugged. "I guess I can always drop out. The most important thing is showing Jason and Rick that they're wrong. Which is why I have to start getting in shape right away. I've got it all planned out. Running, push-ups, sit-ups, aerobics—"

Miranda started laughing. "I can't believe my ears. Can this really be the same Sophie Schultz who practically wanted to throw a party to celebrate when they closed the junior high school gym last year to fix the ceiling?"

I put my chin in the air. "Miranda, this is the beginning of a new me. I'm starting a whole new regimen. I've got exactly eight days until the test, and I'm going to use every spare minute to get ready." To prove how serious I was, I did a couple of deep knee bends right there in front of my locker.

Later that afternoon, in my room at home, I suited up for my first exercise session. I knew I didn't exactly look like a typical jogger in my peace-sign T-shirt and orange flowered boxer shorts, but it was the best I could do. I didn't own anything that looked like real exercise clothes.

Now all I needed were some shoes. I rummaged through the mountain of stuff in the bottom of my closet. I found clogs, sandals, rubber flip-flops, and purple suede platform shoes that I hadn't worn since I twisted my ankle in them over the summer . . . nothing I could really run in, though.

I walked down the hall to Jason's room and opened the door.

Jason was sitting on the edge of his bed shooting a foam basketball into the mini-hoop mounted on the back of his closet door.

"Hey, haven't you ever heard of knocking?" he complained.

I shrugged. "I didn't know you were in here."

He scowled. "Why were you coming into my room, then?"

"I need some sneakers," I explained. "Do you have any that will fit me?"

"Maybe," he said, tossing a ball again.

I sighed. "Well, where are they?"

"Check the closet," he said. "In the back."

I crossed the room to the closet.

"What's with the getup, Soppy?" Jason asked. He snickered. "You look even weirder than usual. What's up? And what do you need my sneakers for, anyway?"

"None of your business," I replied. The last thing I was about to do was to tell Jason about my new exercise program. I knew he'd only make fun of me. I opened the closet door. As I did, I felt the foam basketball hit me on the shoulder.

"Hey!" I heard Jason yell. "Toss that back!"

I ignored him and began looking through the closet. It was pretty disgusting. There was a lot of dirty laundry on the floor, and I even saw a couple of empty candy wrappers. Finally, in the back, I found a pair of old black high-tops that looked smaller than the other shoes. I slipped one on. A little big, but they would have to do. I picked up the sneakers and headed back out of the closet.

"Which ones do you have?" Jason demanded.

I held up the sneakers.

Jason shook his head. "No way. Those are my good-luck sneakers."

"Come on, Jason, you haven't even had these on since seventh grade," I said. "Besides, I'm not going to do anything to them."

"You better not," Jason grumbled.

I rolled my eyes. *As if he even remembered these sneakers before I took them out just now,* I said to myself. But I didn't say anything. The last thing I needed was to start a fight with Jason now. I could end up jogging in my clogs. So I just waved and hurried out of the room.

Outside, the air was hot. It had turned into one of those afternoons that feel more like July than October. I pulled my hair into a ponytail and fastened it with the bright green scrunchie I had on my wrist.

I decided to head for the bike trail, where I'd sometimes noticed people jogging before. The trail starts out by the ferry dock by Cayenga town center, goes up past Mesa Village, the development where I live, and continues through some ranchland to the east before heading into the park. I used to ride it a lot with my friends when I was younger. I hadn't been on it in a while, though, and I'd never taken it on foot. I wasn't sure how long it was, but I figured if I jogged to the park and back that should be a pretty good workout.

I touched my toes a couple of times and then set off.

Jason's big sneakers were kind of flopping on my feet, but other than that I felt pretty good. I took some deep breaths and felt the sunshine on my back.

By the time I was out of Mesa Village and into the ranch area I was starting to feel a little hot and tired. *I guess maybe I should have brought some water or something,* I realized. There were a few trees nearby, and I was tempted to stop and rest in the shade for a while, but I kept going. *Just make it to the park,* I told myself firmly. *Keep going, and don't stop until you get there.*

I also realized I should have brought my CD player with me. Some music would have definitely helped me take my mind off the way I was feeling. Meanwhile, I kept my goal—the park—in my mind and tried not to think about how hot and tired I felt. One of Jason's sneakers was rubbing at the heel a little, and sweat began to drip down my face. But I ignored it all. I was determined to make it to the park without stopping. A couple of people rode by me on bikes and waved. I barely managed to wave back.

Finally, the trail came out beside Route 5 and I began to see large wooden signs for the park's north entrance. I gulped air and pushed myself to keep going. Ten minutes later, I arrived in the dirt parking lot in front of the park's mountain-biking area.

I bent over from the waist and supported my hands on my knees, gasping for air. I had a pain in my side, and I felt like my whole body was on fire. My heart was pounding in my chest.

A moment later, I heard a voice above me. "Is everything all right?"

24

I looked up and saw a woman in a green and gray park uniform.

"Yeah, sure, fine," I managed, still panting. I swallowed. "Is there a water fountain around here?"

"Right over there." The woman nodded toward a small cement building across the parking lot. "Are you sure you're okay?"

I managed to smile. "Fine. Just thirsty. Thanks."

I stumbled across the parking lot to the building and found the water fountain. The water was cold, and it felt great. I took a long drink and then walked into the women's rest room next door. When I saw myself in the mirror above the sink, I realized why the ranger had been worried about me. My face was beet red and I was dripping with sweat. I turned on the faucet and splashed some water on my face.

I was exhausted, and my heel was really starting to hurt me where the sneaker had rubbed. I knew my muscles were going to be aching like crazy tomorrow. But I wasn't about to give up now. I took a deep breath and trotted out toward the trail to jog back home.

FOUR

The night before the test, I sat at the table, staring down at my plate. Usually I love Friday dinners, because my mom picks up Mexican food on her way home from work. But tonight I couldn't touch a bite of my burrito. My stomach was in knots.

Jason, however, was chowing down like this was his last meal for a month.

"Sophie, eat up, hon. It's getting cold," my mother prodded.

I squirmed in my chair. "I guess I'm not really so hungry," I said.

My mother looked concerned. "You're not coming down with something, are you?" She leaned over and put her hand against my forehead. "You don't feel warm."

"I'm not sick, Mom," I told her, wriggling away. To reassure her I reached for a corn chip from the basket in the middle of the table and put it in my mouth.

"Well, it's not like you to lose your appetite," my mother said.

"That's for sure," Jason cracked, wiping guacamole off his mouth with his hand.

"I wouldn't talk if I were you, Jason!" I shot back.

"Wouldn't talk! Ha! That would be a change!" Jason replied.

"Kids, please!" My mother's voice sounded tired. "When will you two learn to get along?"

"Never!" Jason and I said at the same time. Then we both started cracking up. For a minute, it reminded me of when we were little. We were closer back then, and we used to make faces and laugh at the dinner table together all the time. But after my dad left everything changed. We moved to a new neighborhood, and my mom got a full-time job. I'm not sure exactly why, but Jason and I started fighting more then, too.

"Hey, Mom, if Sophie doesn't eat her burrito, can I have it?" Jason asked.

"Sophie is going to eat her dinner," my mother said firmly.

I sighed and picked up my fork. I knew better than to argue with my mom when she used that voice.

"Go ahead, Soppy, eat," Jason said with a grin. "After all, you're going to need all your strength to scale that twenty-foot wall tomorrow."

I almost choked on my food. *Is he serious?* I thought. *Is that part of the test?*

"Jason, what are you talking about?" my mother asked. "What wall?"

"The wall in the junior rangers test," Jason said, still grinning. "And that's the easy part."

I tried not to look worried. "You remember, Mom," I said calmly. "I'm taking the test for the girls' division of the junior rangers tomorrow. I've been working out all week to get ready."

"Oh, of course," my mother said. She wrinkled her forehead. "But are you really going to have to scale a wall? That doesn't sound safe. What if you fall?"

"Don't worry, I won't," I said, trying to sound confident.

"Because you won't even make it up high enough to fall," Jason cracked.

"Jason!" my mother chided. "Remember, in this family we support one another. If Sophie's decided to take this test, I expect you to be cheering her on tomorrow."

"I can't," Jason responded, his mouth full. "No spectators allowed at the tryouts. Park rules."

"Really?" I said hopefully. "You mean nobody's allowed to watch us while we take the test?" *This is good news,* I thought. *The last thing I want is to be humiliated in front of a bunch of people—especially my brother and Rick.*

"I think it's a dumb rule," Jason said.

"Well, did anyone watch *you* when *you* were trying out?" my mother asked him.

Jason shrugged. "No, but . . ."

"Well, then it should be the same for the girls," my mother said firmly. She stood up and began to clear the table.

"If the test *is* the same for the girls," Jason whispered to me when she'd gone, "believe me, you don't stand a chance, Soppy."

I gulped and felt my burrito do a somersault in my stomach. I sure hoped Jason was wrong.

The next morning I decided to jog to the park for the tryouts. Park headquarters was a little closer to my house than the mountain-biking area I had been running to. I thought a short run might be a good way to warm up for the test.

I tied the fraying laces on Jason's old high-tops, pressed PLAY on my CD player, and took off toward the bike path. The sun was low in the sky, and the air was still cool. The sounds of my favorite Derek Jadow CD played in my ears. I felt good.

As I ran, I thought about how much progress I'd made in the past week. Not that jogging to the park and back didn't still make me feel tired. But in the past couple of days I'd been getting a lot less winded. And my legs were feeling stronger, too. I'd actually gotten to the point where I kind of looked forward to my after-school runs each day, especially since I had started wearing my headphones.

Maybe I'll keep this up a few days a week, even after the test is over today, I decided.

Before I knew it, the path was veering off toward the ranch area, and I was directly across the road from the main entrance to the park. I jogged across the crosswalk, into the main parking lot, and toward the small ranger's booth. A man inside in a ranger's uniform was collecting parking fees and waving cars into the lot.

"Hi," I said to the ranger, pressing the STOP button on my CD player. "I'm here for the tryouts. You know, for the junior rangers," I added. I felt kind of funny saying it.

"Oh, sure," he said. "Just head straight along this road right here to the park headquarters building to register."

"Thanks," I said.

"Good luck!" he called after me.

As I made my way along the road under the overhanging trees, I started to get that funny feeling in my stomach again.

Nervousness, I thought. Then I wondered. *Or could it be excitement?*

For the first time all week, I realized I couldn't tell!

CARSON

FIVE

Run, run, run, run, run, run, run, jump! Run, run, run, run, run, run, run, jump! Run, run, run, run, run, run, run, jump! I tried to keep the rhythm of the track and the hurdles in my mind as I ran. I'd already cleared the first five hurdles; only three more to go to make it a perfect run. I breathed evenly and kept my elbows in toward my sides. I could feel my thick, blonde braid bumping against my neck as I ran.

Run, run, run, run, run, run, run, jump! Run, run, run, run, run, run, run, jump! Run, run, run, run, run, run, run, run, ooops! At the last hurdle I felt my rhythm go. I was sightly late with my back leg, and my foot brushed the hurdle on the way over, toppling it. I took the final steps to the finish and turned, jogging in place, to check the course. Sure enough, the first seven hurdles were still standing, and the last one had fallen.

I glanced up at Coach Calhoun, and she gave me a thumbs-up sign.

I shook my head. "I hit one," I said, walking toward her.

"But you made good time," she said. She turned her stopwatch to show me.

Seventeen point six seconds. It was true that I had beat my last time by three tenths of a second. *But that's not good enough if you have to knock over a hurdle to do it,* I reminded myself. *Remember, if this were a meet, you'd be penalized for that.*

I felt Coach Calhoun's arm on my shoulder, and I turned to face her.

"You're too hard on yourself sometimes, Carson," she said. "Take it easy."

I wiped the sweat off my forehead and grinned. I knew she was right. I'm definitely the toughest coach around when it comes to my own performance. But I also know you've got to be tough if you want to be the best you can.

Coach put her whistle to her mouth and blew. "That's it for today, girls!" she called. "See you Tuesday morning for practice again. And don't forget, we have a meet against Sunshine County High next Friday. Have a good weekend, everybody."

I jogged across the field toward the locker room with the rest of the track team.

Jessie Marconi ran up alongside me. Her face was glistening with sweat, and her dark bangs were plastered down on her forehead. "I still say there ought to be a law against holding a practice this early on a Saturday morning," she complained. "I mean, weekends are supposed to be for sleeping late, aren't they?"

I shrugged, and we slowed to a walk. "I guess." I laughed. "Even without early practice there isn't much hope of sleeping late at my house, though. Not with five brothers and sisters running around getting ready for tennis lessons, swim practice, and soccer."

Jessie shook her head. "You McDonalds might as well start your own sports complex over there. You know, sell memberships and stuff."

"No thanks!" I groaned. "We only have three bathrooms, and they're already crowded enough as it is!"

Jessie laughed as we walked into the locker-room facility.

"Catch you later, Jess," I said.

"See you, Carson," she replied.

We headed our separate ways toward our gym lockers. Ashley Cho, who has the locker next to mine, was already there, combing through her short black hair.

"Hey, Carson, you made nice time today," Ashley commented.

"Thanks," I answered, pulling the rubber band off my braid. "You looked pretty good out there, too. I missed a hurdle that last time, though. Hopefully we'll all get it together for the meet against Sunshine on Friday."

"Yeah, I heard Sunshine's pretty good." Ashley said, turning toward her locker.

I spun my combination lock and opened my locker. As I reached inside to get my shampoo, I just caught the end of something Ashley was saying. You see, I have a hearing disability. I have no hearing in my left ear, and only some hearing in my right. Even with my hearing aid,

I can't always understand what people are saying to me unless I can watch their mouths and read their lips while they're talking. Since Ashley had her head turned away from me, I'd missed part of what she had said.

"I didn't catch that, Ash," I said.

"Oh, sorry," Ashley apologized. "I was just asking you if you were going to the park to try out for the junior rangers today."

"Definitely," I said. "I'd been looking forward to the Cayenga Park junior ranger tryouts all week. My mom is a park ranger. "You're going too, right?"

"I'm not sure," Ashley answered.

"You should," I urged her. "It'll be fun."

"Did your mom tell you anything about the qualifying test?" Ashley asked. "I've heard it's really hard."

"She can't be one of the test administrators this year, since I'm trying out," I explained. "But I don't think it'll be too hard. I'm pretty sure it's just the same test they usually give the boys. My brother Logan was a junior ranger for three years. He said it was really fun. You should definitely give it a shot."

Ashley shrugged. "Okay, why not? I guess I'll wait until after the tryouts to shower. I mean what's the sense if I'm just going to get all dirty and sweaty again?"

"I'm going to shower anyway," I said. I kind of have this thing about showers. Not that I mind getting sweaty. But I do like to shower after I exercise, even if I am going to break a sweat again soon. With all the teams and sports I'm involved in, sometimes I feel like I spend half my life sweating and the other half showering!

I grabbed a clean towel from the bin by the wall. "Catch you later at the tryouts, Ashley!" I called.

She waved.

I checked the clock. Nine o'clock. I had just enough time to shower and stop home for breakfast before going to the park.

As I rode my bike up the driveway to my house, I took a deep breath of sea air. I love living by the water. Our house isn't on the beach, like some of those fancy places over by Cayenga Heights. But it's only two streets down from the Cayenga boat basin, and the air always smells salty and cool.

The only cars in the driveway were the van and my dad's truck, so I knew my mom had probably already taken the old station wagon to work. Saturdays and Sundays are some of the busiest days over at Cayenga Park, which is why rangers don't usually end up having weekends off like everyone else. My dad works a lot of weekends, too. He's a football coach over at Cayenga Community College, so his schedule gets pretty hectic during the playing season.

I leaned my bike with the others against the wall in the garage and headed into the house. My dad and my older brother Logan were sitting at the big kitchen table with plates of eggs in front of them. My dad was drawing something on a paper napkin, and he and Logan were studying it intently. Logan's short, blond hair was wet, which meant he had probably already been to swim practice and had a shower.

"Hi, Dad. Hi, Logan." I went to the refrigerator and took out a jug of orange juice.

"Hi, Carson," Logan said. "You have track this morning?"

I nodded. I took out a glass and poured myself some juice.

My father looked up from his napkin. "Hey there, Carson. You hungry? Want me to make you an omelet?"

I shook my head. "That's okay." I sat down at the table with them. "Where is everybody?"

"Mom took Cody and Dakota to tennis on her way to work," Logan offered.

Cody and Dakota are my twelve-year-old brother and sister. They're twins. I should explain that all the kids in our family are named after famous places in the West. For instance, I'm named after Carson City, the capital of Nevada.

The whole name thing started back before we were born, when my mom and dad went on their honeymoon. They drove around the country, camping out. That's when my mom got the idea she wanted to be a park ranger. And they both agreed that the nicest places they saw were in the western part of the country. So they named all six of us kids after western cities and towns. There's Logan, me, the twins, my little sister Cheyenne, and my little brother Jasper. My dad likes to joke that he and my mom stopped having kids because they ran out of good names. He says if there had been one more of us they might have had to name it Tucson or Las Vegas.

My father glanced at his watch. "Cheyenne and Jasper

better get down here and eat breakfast if they want to make it to soccer on time." He picked up his pen again. "Let me just show you the rest of this play, though, Logan. It's the one the Forty-Niners used against the Cowboys in that last game."

My father is always talking to Logan about football, diagramming plays for him, explaining strategies, whatever. Sometimes I wonder if my dad ever notices that Logan doesn't ever have much to say about it himself. The truth is, I don't think Logan's really interested in football at all. Swimming is pretty much Logan's life. He's captain of the boys' team at school, and he wants to go to college in the East next year on a special swimming scholarship. He'd even like to make it to the Olympics one day. I guess he lets my dad talk football to him because he doesn't want to disappoint him.

Just then I felt heavy rhythmic vibrations on the floor under my feet.

"Here come Jasper and Cheyenne, Dad," I said. A couple of moments later, my little sister and brother ran into the room.

"Carson!" Cheyenne gave me a hug. She stepped back to let me see her face. "Want to see me do a handstand?"

I laughed. "Not in the kitchen, Cheyenne! How about later on, outside?" Lately Cheyenne's been totally into gymnastics.

Cheyenne looked disappointed. "Well, okay. What's for breakfast?"

"How about omelets?" my dad asked.

Cheyenne wrinkled her nose and stuck out her tongue. "How bout Coco-Mocho cereal?"

"Yeah!" Jasper agreed. He pulled a kitchen chair over to the counter and climbed up on the counter. He opened up the cabinet and pulled out a box of cereal with a picture of a brown cartoon rabbit on it. "I get the prize!"

"No, I get it!" Cheyenne objected.

"No way. I got the box down so I get the prize," Jasper said, hugging the cereal to his chest.

"No fair!" Cheyenne was almost in tears.

"Jasper, just because you got the box down doesn't automatically mean you get the prize," I said.

"See?" Cheyenne said.

"But it doesn't mean you get it, either," I told my sister. "Both of you sit down and I'll pour you some cereal. If the prize comes out in your bowl, it's yours."

Jasper and Cheyenne scrambled to their seats.

Logan chuckled. "Dad, maybe you'd better start putting prizes in your omelets."

My father laughed, too. "Good idea. Maybe that way I'd finally get some takers."

"I'd love to have an omelet, Dad, really. But I have to go to ranger tryouts at the park," I said. "I don't want to eat anything too heavy beforehand."

"Oh, right," my dad replied. "Hey, good luck today, Carson."

"Yeah, go for it, Cars," Logan echoed. He flashed me the hand signs for "good luck." Everyone in my family knows some sign language. I learned it when I was little to help me communicate, and the rest of the family picked up a bunch of it, too.

"Thanks," I signed back to Logan. I poured some

cereal into Jasper's and Cheyenne's bowls. "See? *Nobody* got the prize. Now you'll just both have to wait until next time." I sighed. *I guess the cereal companies don't exactly have big families like ours in mind when they put those prizes in their boxes,* I thought.

I made some toast with cream cheese and served myself some fruit salad from the refrigerator. I sat down at the table next to Cheyenne, who was happily munching her Coco-Mocho.

Logan stood up and brought his plate over to the sink. "Well, see you all later. Good luck with the game today, Dad."

"Wait! Logan, can you give me a ride to the park?" I asked.

"If you think you can be ready in five minutes," he answered. "I promised Mom I'd pick up the twins after their lesson."

"No problem," I said, quickly scooping some fruit salad into my mouth. "We can stop and get them on the way."

"You two hurry up and finish, too," my father instructed Jasper and Cheyenne. "We've got to leave for soccer soon." He grinned. "It's another complicated Saturday in the McDonald household, but we've got it under control. Sometimes I think it's the *pro teams* who should be studying the *McDonald* game plans and strategies, instead of the other way around."

We all laughed.

SIX

A little while later I sat next to Ashley Cho on the grass in front of the Park Headquarters and filled out my form to register for the tryouts.

There were about twenty-five girls there, sitting in the grass filling out their forms.

Ashley nudged me. "Hey, look. It's that new girl from school."

I followed her gaze across the lawn and recognized a petite, wiry girl with short dark hair and deep green eyes. She wasn't in any of my classes, but I knew she was in tenth grade, like me. I had noticed her right away at the beginning of the year. How could I not, when she was the only girl at Cayenga High with a nose ring? Well, it wasn't exactly a *ring*. It was more of a stud, tiny and silver. But it was still pretty unusual-looking, especially for Cayenga.

Ashley screwed up her face. "I would never wear a thing in my nose like that."

CALIFORNIA STATE PARKS
CAYENGA COUNTY REGION
CAYENGA PARK

APPLICATION FOR RANGER UNIT LEARNING EXTENSION

NAME: _Carson McDonald_ TEL: _555-1945_

ADDRESS: _2205 Harbor Way, Cayenga, California_

HOW DID YOU LEARN ABOUT THE LEARNING EXTENSION?

My mom is a Cayenga Park ranger!!

AGE: _15_ SCHOOL: _Cayenga High School_ GRADE: _10_

FOR CAYENGA PARK ADMINISTRATION ONLY:

DATE TESTED: _____

SCORES:

STRENGTH: _____ AGILITY: _____ SPEED/ENDURANCE: _____

PARK TEST: _____ MEMORY: _____ OBSTACLE COURSE: _____

TOTAL SCORE: _____

_____ PASS _____ FAIL

I shrugged. "I heard she's from New York," I said. "Maybe that's the style there."

"Maybe," Ashley echoed. "Hey, isn't that other girl behind her in our ceramics class?"

Sure enough, sitting a little farther off was a girl with long red hair and freckles whom I recognized from ceramics.

"Hey yeah," I said. I waved to the girl, but she was looking the other way and didn't notice.

"What's she doing here?" Ashley wondered.

I shrugged. "Trying out, I guess."

"Yeah, I guess," Ashley echoed. "I just didn't think she was the type. I mean, she's not on any teams at school or anything, right?"

"I don't think so," I replied. "Not that she has to be on a team to want to work in the park," I added. Still, I knew what Ashley meant. The red-haired girl didn't seem like the athletic type, somehow. It was hard to imagine her as a junior ranger.

Still, it's never a good idea to judge a book by its cover, I reminded myself. *Remember, when you first got to the high school there were coaches who thought you couldn't ever be the captain of a team because of your hearing. They said you'd never be able to lead and communicate with the rest of the team during a game. But you proved them wrong.*

I turned to Ashley. "You never know. Maybe she's not the team type, but she could still be the outdoors type. She might make a good junior ranger."

"Maybe." But the expression on Ashley's face still looked doubtful.

Right then and there I made up my mind to give the red-haired girl a chance before I jumped to any conclusions about her. *After all,* I reasoned, *I don't like it when people make assumptions about what I can and can't do.*

Just then, a man I recognized as Ranger Abe Mayfield, my mom's boss, stood up in front of the group. I fixed my eyes on his face.

"Welcome, everyone," he began. "I'm Ranger Mayfield, but everybody here at the park calls me Ranger Abe. I'm glad to see you all here today. We'll begin the test in just a couple of minutes. First I want to introduce the rangers who are going to be administering the test and keeping track of your scores. They are Ranger Janet Lord and Ranger Michael Loukowsky."

A man and a woman in rangers' uniforms came over and stood beside him.

"The exam you are about to take is to help us determine which of you might have the necessary qualities to join the Learning Extension, or the junior rangers," Ranger Abe continued. "The test will be a challenge for all of you; each time we give it we have many fine applicants who do not pass. Of course, if you don't pass this time, you'll have the opportunity to try again sometime down the line."

I could feel my heart start to beat faster with excitement, the way it always does before a meet or a game.

"The exam will be made up of several sections, or subtests," Ranger Abe went on. "In the end, it will be your total score on these tests that will determine which of you will make it to the Learning Extension. If you have any problems during the testing, or if you have any special concerns, please let the other rangers or myself know."

I knew Ranger Abe probably already knew about my disability, from my mom. But the rangers who were giving the test probably didn't know anything about me. And I wasn't going to say anything. I kind of like to keep that part of me private. There are a lot of people at school who don't even know about it.

I want to be judged exactly the same way as everyone else taking the test, I reasoned. *I don't want anyone to think I'm getting special treatment. Hopefully if I pay attention and watch the rangers' faces, I won't have too much trouble following the directions.*

We all stood up and followed the rangers out to the testing area behind the headquarters building. As I thought about the challenge ahead of me I could feel my heart pounding harder than ever with anticipation. I wiped my palms on my shorts and took a deep breath.

Ashley nudged me. "Good luck, McDonald," she said with a grin. She held up her hand.

"Good luck, Cho," I replied, giving her a high five.

Half an hour later my whole body was trembling with effort as I clung to a chin-up bar in a bent-arm hang. I knew I'd already scored well in the early portions of the test—sit-ups, push-ups, and squat-thrusts. In fact, so far the test was pretty easy, nothing more than a basic gym class at school.

Now I was determined to boost my score some more in

the bent-arm hang. Ignoring the aching muscles in my upper arms, I breathed evenly and used every bit of my concentration to keep my position steady.

Every few seconds I could feel a vibration in the bar under my hands as another girl gave up and dropped to the ground with a thump. I continued concentrating, resisting the urge to glance to either side of me to see how many girls were left.

Your strongest competition is always against yourself, I reminded myself. *Don't waste energy wondering how other people are doing. Just concentrate on your own performance, and do the best you can do.*

Finally, my arms just couldn't hold out any longer. I released my hands and dropped to the ground. Ranger Lord nodded at me encouragingly as she noted my time on her clipboard.

I stretched out my aching arms and looked around. Only one girl was still hanging from the bar. Her body was shaking from effort just like mine had been, and I noticed sweat glistening on her dark legs below her white shorts. When she finally dropped to the ground a few moments later and wiped her face with her arm, I noticed she looked familiar.

At first I wasn't sure why. She didn't go to our school, I knew that. Then I remembered where I knew her from—the Harmon track team. Harmon Academy is a girls' school in Cayenga. We don't usually compete against them, because they're a private school. But a couple of years ago, when I was in eighth grade at Rio Verde Junior High, the county organized a "Youth Olympics." All the teams from all the schools in the area competed in swimming, gymnastics, and track-and-field events. This girl on the Harmon team stuck in my mind. She was really limber and strong, even back then. I remember a lot of her running times beat some of the high school times, even though she was only in seventh grade at the time.

I caught her eye and gave her a friendly smile. She smiled back, but I couldn't tell if she remembered who I was. The thing about me is that I never forget a face. Maybe it's because I don't hear voices very well. So I try to concentrate on other things, like the way things—or people—look. This girl had high cheekbones, brown, sloping, almond-shaped eyes, smooth brown skin, and thick shoulder-length black hair. There was something about the intense look in her eyes that made me think that a lot of people who saw her didn't forget her too easily.

Just then Ashley walked over to me. With her was Kim Cryer, who's on the volleyball team with me.

"I did really badly on that last test," Ashley said. "I have no upper-body strength. All my power is in my legs."

Kim grinned. "That's what happens when you run track, Ashley. You've got to play volleyball if you want strong arms. Right, Carson?"

I shrugged. "Yeah, I guess track isn't the greatest for upper body." Then I had a thought. *I wonder how that girl from Harmon developed such strong arms. She must do something else besides run track, too.*

My thoughts were interrupted as I noticed that Ranger

Loukowsky was speaking, starting to give us our next instructions. I focused on what he was saying.

"That concludes the strength portion of the test," he said. "If you'll all come this way, we'll start the agility test."

"Agility—that's like coordination, right?" Kim asked. "I wonder how they're going to test us for that."

Ashley laughed. "Maybe they'll ask us to pat our heads while we rub our stomachs or something."

I laughed, too. Then I spotted something that made me stop laughing. It was a tire run, a double row of tires tied together and placed on the ground. It looked just like the one the football teams worked out with at school. My dad says running through a tire run is a great way to get players to develop their footwork. It takes a lot of precision to place your feet in the tires at each step and not get tripped up. My dad says he tells his players it's either that or take ballet classes. Most of the guys choose the tire run.

The thing is, even though I'm pretty strong and I'm pretty fast, fancy footwork has never been one of my best areas. I can hit a softball out of the park, or sprint a mile with no problem, but I know I'd be lost in a ballet class. And I had a feeling I wasn't going to be so great at the tire run either.

Just do your best, I reminded myself as I lined up by the tires with the rest of the group. *Remember, you already have some pretty high scores. You'll probably still do fine overall even if you don't score near the top on this one.*

My turn finally came, and I gazed down at the tire run, trying not to feel intimidated by it. Ranger Loukowsky gave me the signal to start, and I made my way down the double row, taking care to place my feet solidly in each one of the tires in turn. When I finished, I knew I hadn't made great time, but I'd done okay. And at least I hadn't tripped over the tires and fallen. That could have cost me a lot of time.

Just as I finished, I noticed a figure in the distance, among the trees. Whoever it was had his or her arms bent, elbows out at an angle. The person shifted slightly, and I saw the glint of a reflection off the face. *Binoculars,* I realized with surprise. *Someone is standing over there in the woods watching us with binoculars! But who? And why?*

Just then my attention was caught by the new girl from school, the one I'd heard was from New York. It was her turn to navigate the tire run, and she was doing an amazing job. She was practically dancing through the double row of tires, placing her feet in each one of the tires and removing them again at lightning speed. There was something really graceful about the way she moved, too, almost like a deer. I saw the long muscles of her legs flexing beneath her black bicycle shorts as she moved. I also noticed that she wore a special elastic support on her left knee, as if she had an old injury. Still, in spite of whatever injury she might have had, she made the tire run look so easy! I was impressed.

I smiled at her as she finished. "That was great," I commented.

"Thanks," she said. "I have one of these tire things at home in my room, so I get a lot of practice."

I stared at her. "You do?"

She grinned. "No, I was just kidding. Actually, I used to do a lot of gymnastics. Running through those tires almost seems easy compared to leaping across a balance beam, believe me."

"I bet," I replied.

"I'm Becca," she offered. "Becca Fisher."

"Hi, Becca," I said. "I'm Carson."

"I know," she said. "Carson McDonald. Everybody knows who you are."

"Really?" I said with surprise.

"Sure. They make all the new students take a class, Carson McDonald 101. Didn't you know?" She laughed. "Just kidding."

I laughed too, but I couldn't help wondering about what she had said. *I guess it's true that I have a lot of friends at school,* I realized, *mostly from all the teams I'm on. I guess that's what Becca meant.* I wondered what it would be like to be new, and if Becca had made any friends yet.

The last of the girls finished up the tire run, and Ranger Lord announced the next portion of the exam—a test for speed and endurance.

"We'll be timing you as you make the run along the trail that leads up by Rattlesnake Canyon to the river and back," she explained. "Ranger Loukowsky has already taken a vehicle up that way, and he will be waiting for you at the river checkpoint. Make sure you go directly to him when you get there. He will give you an orange ticket as proof that you made it to the checkpoint. After that, turn around and run back here, and I will mark your total time."

I mentally computed the distance to the point at which the Rattlesnake Canyon trail met the river. *Probably about three quarters of a mile,* I decided. *Which would make the whole run about a mile and a half. Not exactly a sprint, but still a short enough distance that I can pretty much turn on some speed right away and not have to worry too much about pacing myself.* I was pretty confident that I'd be able to score well enough in the speed test to make up for whatever I'd lost in the tire run.

I turned and followed the group as they made for the head of the trail. As we left the tire-run area, I suddenly remembered the figure I had noticed earlier watching us from the woods. I swiveled to take another look, still curious about who it might be.

But the woods were empty now. Whoever it was had vanished.

SEVEN

Later, I sat in the main meeting room of the ranger headquarters and stared at the piece of paper in front of me. I tried to concentrate.

What was that last item? I asked myself. The rangers had shown us a tray with fifteen different things on it, and now that the tray was gone we were supposed to try to write down as many of the items as we could remember in one minute. Since I've always worked hard at noticing things and remembering what I've seen, I was able to think of the first ten items from the tray pretty easily. But the last few had taken some effort. And this very last one had me stumped. *What could it be?*

I glanced around briefly at the other girls. Most of them were busy writing. The red-haired girl from ceramics had her eyes squeezed shut, as if she were thinking really hard. The girl from the Harmon track team was bent over her paper, scribbling furiously. Beside her I spotted another girl, with straight, silky, shoulder-length

```
MEMORY TEST:

NAME: Carson McDonald

1. rock            6. leaf              11. jack-knife

2 key              7 Cayenga Park       12. matches
                     post card
3. eraser          8. sunglasses        13. ranger badge

4. pen             9. string            14. shell

5. watch          10. compass          15.
```

light brown hair, sitting patiently, her big brown eyes calmly gazing around the room. Her hands were folded on the overturned paper on her lap. I stared at her. *Is she finished? Did she remember all the items already?* I wondered. *Or did she just give up?*

I glanced at Ranger Loukowsky, who was timing us with his stopwatch. I turned back to my paper.

Paper! I thought suddenly. *That's it!* I bent over and scribbled the last item.

15. paper clip

"Time's up!" Ranger Loukowsky announced.

I breathed a sigh of relief. *That last one was just in time,* I thought as I handed my paper to the ranger.

A few minutes later, the scores were in. It turned out

that only two girls had correctly remembered all fifteen items. Me, and the girl with the light brown hair I had noticed.

"That's totally phenomenal, Carson," Kim Cryer commented, looking at my paper. "How'd you do that? I only remembered nine things."

"I only got eight!" Ashley complained.

Kim sighed. "I don't think I'm doing so well. I also missed three questions on that park-knowledge test we did before this one."

"I did okay on that one," Ashley said. "But between this memory thing and that trick they played on us with the orange tickets after the trail race, I'm sunk."

"Well, it wasn't exactly a *trick,* Ashley," I objected. What had happened was that the rangers had added bonus points to the score of any girl who kept her ticket until she could throw it in a trash bin, as I did. Anyone who dropped her ticket on the ground or left it somewhere in the park got points taken away. "I think they were just trying to give extra points for remembering to keep the park clean," I said.

"Yeah, well, I would have remembered to keep the park clean if they'd reminded me," Ashley grumbled. "How many more parts are there to this test anyway?"

"Well, let's see," I said, thinking back to the registration form we'd filled out earlier that morning. "We've done strength, agility, speed and endurance, the park test, memory. . . . I think all that's left is the obstacle course."

The obstacle course turned out to be in a special area

by the campgrounds. The rangers had set up a series of challenges for us to go through in pairs.

Ranger Lord explained what we were supposed to do. "Each pair of girls will start by climbing the net to this platform," she said, indicating a wooden platform about ten feet off the ground with a large net hanging down one side. "Next, you'll use this rope to swing to the next platform, and from there you'll cross the beam to the third platform." She indicated a narrow wooden beam suspended high in the air.

I scanned the crowd and located Becca. I wasn't too surprised to see her grinning from ear to ear at the sight of the balance beam. She caught my eye and flashed me the thumbs-up sign. I smiled back at her.

Ranger Lord finished explaining the obstacle course. After the beam, we were supposed to jump into a sandpile and then sprint thirty yards to a large wall. Attached to the top of the wall, which looked about fifteen feet high, were two thick ropes that dangled down the surface. We were supposed to climb the wall by pulling ourselves up by the ropes, and then run down a sharply angled ramp on the other side.

"After that," Ranger Lord said with a small smile, "all you have to do is find your way back to park headquarters. The choice is yours: you can take the main road, which circles around down by the cove, or you can find a shorter route on your own with your partner, using a compass and navigating the park's backcountry. Just remember that you're being timed."

It doesn't make any sense to take the main road, I

thought. *It's much longer. The woods between here and park headquarters are pretty dense, but even so, it'll be much faster to go that way, especially with a compass.*

I felt Kim's hand on my arm. "Carson, be my partner, okay? I don't know the park that well, so I really need someone like you to help me with the end part."

I was about to reply when I realized that Ranger Loukowsky was talking. I turned and focused on what he was saying.

"In order to keep things fair, we are assigning the partners randomly. Please listen for your name and find your partner." He began to read from a list. "Becca Fisher and Kayla Adams." Kayla Adams turned out to be the girl I remembered from the Harmon track team. I watched as she and Becca paired off, and then turned my attention back to Ranger Loukowsky. He continued down the list and finally read my name. "Carson McDonald and Sophie Schultz."

"Oh well," Kim said with a sigh.

"I'm sure you'll do okay, Kim," I said, smiling encouragingly. I looked around for my partner. *Sophie Schultz? That name sounds familiar somehow, but . . .*

Suddenly the red-haired girl from ceramics was standing in front of me.

"Sophie?" I asked.

She nodded. "Hi, Carson. I guess we're partners." She fidgeted a little nervously with a lock of her red hair.

"Great," I said with a smile.

A look of relief crossed Sophie's face. "Really?"

"Sure." I hesitated, thinking, and then made my

decision. "But there's something I have to tell you about first, something you should know about if we're going to work together and rely on each other," I said. I cleared my throat. "I have some trouble with my hearing, a disability. I can hear some things, but it helps if I can read your lips when you're talking, too. It doesn't have to be a big deal. It just means that I'll understand you better if I can see your face when you talk to me."

Sophie nodded. "Okay, sure, no problem." She paused. "Actually, I should tell you something, too."

"What is it?" I asked.

She looked embarrassed. "Well, it's just that I haven't really done anything like this before. I mean, I guess you can probably guess that I'm not a jock or anything." She grinned. "In fact, I only started working out a week ago. So I might not be the greatest partner in the world. But I promise I'll try as hard as I possibly can, and no matter what, I won't give up. Still, I understand if you want to go ask the rangers for a new partner. I mean, I don't want to hurt your chances or anything."

Looking at her, I couldn't help admiring her. Her red hair was plastered to her head with sweat, and she had dirt streaks on her face. Her pale, freckled face was still red from the exertion of the earlier tests.

"You know what, Sophie?" I said. "You're just the kind of person I'd choose to have on my team for this part of the test."

"Really?" Her eyes widened in surprise.

"Definitely," I told her. "For something like an obstacle course it's really important to work with someone who's ready to give one hundred percent." I grinned. "From what I can tell, you seem like the kind of person who doesn't let any obstacles stand in her way."

Sophie smiled, and her whole face lit up. "Okay, Carson, you're on," she said. "Let's give it all we've got."

Ten minutes later it was our turn for the obstacle course. I stood by Sophie, fingering the compass on the string around my neck as I watched Ranger Loukowsky's face for the sign to begin.

"Go!"

The moment his mouth formed the word I felt Sophie's hand touch my arm as a signal. We both took off toward the net that led to the first platform.

For a moment I was ahead of Sophie as we clawed our way up the net. But at the last minute my sneaker got caught in one of the holes, so we made it to the top and climbed onto the first platform at the same moment.

"Here!" I reached out for the two ropes and tossed one Sophie's way.

She hesitated a moment.

"Don't look down!" I called to her. "Just swing!"

I clutched my rope and swung out in the air, wrapping my feet around the bottom. As the second platform came within my reach, I grabbed one of its supporting poles. I pulled myself onto the platform and released the rope. Sophie was right behind me. I reached out for her and she grabbed my hand. I pulled her toward the platform.

The balance beam was next. Just looking at the narrow beam and the ten-foot drop below it made my stomach do a flip-flop. I took a deep breath and stepped out onto it.

Easy does it, I reminded myself. *Don't rush too much. One false step and you'll fall and lose a lot of time.* Carefully, with my arms out at my sides for balance, I placed one foot in front of the other until finally I reached the end and stepped onto the third platform.

I turned to face Sophie. She was frozen at the other end of the beam, staring at the ground below.

"Come on, Sophie, you can do it!" I urged.

She bit her lip.

"Remember, a hundred percent!" I said to her. "We're a team. Don't let me down."

She nodded briefly and set her jaw in a determined expression. I saw her take a deep breath. Then, to my surprise, she took off across the beam, practically jogging as she stared fixedly ahead. She was across it in seconds.

I stared at her in amazement.

She shrugged. "I wanted to get it over with," she explained. She tugged on my arm. "Come on, let's go."

Together we leapt into the sandpile below. We stood, shook the sand off, and ran toward the climbing wall. I reached it first and grabbed hold of a rope.

Holding the rope firmly in my hands, I braced my feet against the surface of the wall. Hand over hand, I pulled my way up the wall, bending my knees and keeping my feet wide for support.

My eyes darted to my left to check for Sophie, but she wasn't in sight. Finally, when I reached the top of the wall, I turned and looked down. Sophie was about a third of the way up the wall. Her face was bright red and the expression on her face was twisted with effort.

"Go ahead, Carson!" she called. "Don't wait for me!"

I shook my head. "No way, Sophie! We're a team!"

Sophie managed to pull herself up another few steps, but then her feet slipped and she fell back a bit.

"Go!" she insisted. "You'll make better time without me."

"Sophie, listen to me," I said. "Don't think about the wall. Just think about the rope. Think of pulling the rope toward you, one hand at a time."

Sophie moved her hands along the rope and slowly began to make progress up the wall.

"That's it!" I said to her. "That's right! One hand at a time. Just keep pulling the rope toward you! Don't give up!"

At the words "give up," a hard expression came into Sophie's eyes. She began to climb more quickly.

"You're doing it! You're doing it!" I cried. "You did it!" I threw my arms around her as she climbed to the top of the wall.

Sophie grinned. She grabbed my arm. "Come on!"

We ran down the ramp together. At the bottom, I pulled the string and the compass from inside my T-shirt. Sophie and I had already agreed to take the backcountry route to headquarters.

"Hurry!" Sophie urged. "I just heard the ranger give the signal for the next pair to start the course!"

I studied the compass. *Headquarters should be directly northeast of where we are,* I reasoned. "This way!" I told Sophie.

We took off through the woods. As I had expected, the

trees soon became dense. Sophie and I were forced to clear the lower branches out of our way to get through.

The branches got thicker and thicker. It took both of us working together to clear even a tiny path. I felt like the forest was swallowing us up.

Sophie put her hand on my shoulder. I turned and saw that her cheek had been scratched by a twig.

"Carson, are you sure this is the way?" she asked. "Are you positive we wouldn't be better off on the main road?"

"The main road's way too long," I told her. "Besides, we should be coming out of this soon. There's a canyon they use for rock climbing directly behind park headquarters."

Sophie's eyes widened. "Rock climbing?"

"Don't worry," I told her as we continued pushing our way through the woods. "If we stay slightly to the west of it we'll hit the edge of the canyon where it begins, at its lowest point. Besides, when we reach it we'll be going down, not up. Technically, park headquarters is in a small valley."

Sure enough, a few moments later the forest began to thin out. We ran through the trees, trying not to trip over roots and rocks. I glanced at Sophie. Her face was glowing, and she was breathing heavily. But she was still giving it everything she had. I kept running.

Finally, we cleared the woods and came to the edge of the canyon. At its western end, where we were, the canyon wall was only about twenty feet high. The grade wasn't too steep, but I knew it could be slippery in spots.

"Watch out for loose rocks on your way down," I

warned Sophie. I glanced down at her shoes—a pair of black high-tops that looked like they'd seen better days. "And be careful not to twist your ankle. Those sneakers don't give you much support. You'd be a lot better off with hiking boots."

"Believe me, I know," Sophie gasped, still trying to catch her breath. "If I do make it to the junior rangers the first thing I'm going to do is buy some."

Together we started off down the canyon wall. It was tough going, and at times the only way to keep from falling was to crab-walk down the incline, on our backs. As we made our way lower, the air cooled, and I could smell the moisture of the stream down below. I knew that the stream wouldn't be too high at this time of year, and I figured Sophie and I shouldn't have too much trouble crossing it.

But when we got to the bottom, Sophie regarded the stream doubtfully. I looked at her shoes again and realized what she was thinking. My hiking boots would keep me dry, but Sophie's canvas shoes weren't going to be any good at all in that stream. Even though the water was only about ten inches deep, she was going to get soaked right through her sneakers.

"I could piggy-back you across," I offered.

Sophie shook her head. "You might slip." She shrugged. "Anyway, what's the big deal about a little water?" She moved toward the edge of the stream.

"Are you sure?" I asked her. "It's pretty cold."

Sophie turned to face me. "No problem!" But as she stepped into the water, I saw her wince. "Yow! That's freezing! Come on, Carson!" she urged. "Let's hurry!"

Together we splashed our way through the stream.

"Okay," I said. "Park headquarters should be just over there, through those trees." I glanced at Sophie, who was shivering. "Are you okay?"

"Fine," she insisted. "Let's go!"

But just then, something caught my eye. Something glittering and metallic lying several yards away, in the grass. I moved closer for a better look.

Sophie put her hand on my arm. "Come on, Carson! We're losing time!"

"Wait." I stared at the object in the grass, suddenly realizing what it was. "Look! Over there!" I said. "It's a trap!"

"A trap?" Sophie started toward it. "What kind of trap?"

"The kind for trapping animals," I answered. "And it's the worst type, too—a leghold trap. They're incredibly painful."

"That's awful!" Sophie said.

"It's illegal, too," I replied. "There's no trapping or hunting of any kind allowed in the park. Who would do something like this?"

"Carson, right after the test we can report this to the rangers," Sophie said. "Right now we have to get moving, or we're going to lose too much time."

I knew Sophie was right. Still, I hated to think that while we were completing the obstacle course a rabbit or a raccoon or a deer might come along and get stuck in this trap. Then I had an idea.

I looked around and picked up a big stick. I walked

over to the trap and carefully placed the stick down in the center of it. Immediately the jaws of the trap snapped shut, breaking the stick.

Sophie looked horrified. "Is that what it does to the animal's leg?" she asked.

I nodded. "Sometimes. Sometimes the animal even chews its own leg off to get itself free." Just thinking about it made me feel sick.

Sophie's eyes were fiery. "Who would do something like that? I think whoever set this trap ought to have their own leg snapped off in one!"

I couldn't have agreed more. "That's exactly why I want to be a junior ranger," I explained. "So I can help protect the park and its wildlife from people like this." Then I realized something. "Hey, we'd better get going right away or neither one of us will have a chance to work with the rangers."

"You're right!" Sophie agreed. "Come on!"

We turned away from the trap and ran as fast as we could toward park headquarters.

BECCA

EIGHT

"Wheee!" I let out a yell as I swung out on the rope into the air.

Finally, I thought happily, *we've come to a part of the test that's really fun.* Not that I hated all the push-ups and sit-ups and stuff. They were okay. But going through this obstacle course was like being a kid back in the playground in Central Park again.

I glanced over at my partner, a girl named Kayla with dark hair, brown skin, and deep orange-brown eyes that reminded me of a tiger's—or, rather, what I thought a tiger's would look like up close. I've never actually been face-to-face with a real tiger.

I was pretty sure Kayla didn't go to my new school, but I'd only been there a month, and there were a lot of students. It was possible I just hadn't noticed her. My old school, in New York, was really small compared to Cayenga High. Which is why sometimes school in California felt more like college to me. I mean, Cayenga has *two* football teams! My old school in New York didn't even have *one*!

Kayla had a really serious expression on her face, the same expression she'd had since we started the obstacle course together. Not that I wasn't serious about passing the test for the junior park rangers. But somehow it seemed kind of hard to takes things too seriously when you were swinging through the air on a rope.

Kayla and I reached the second platform together, and I grinned. "Hey, fancy meeting you here," I joked.

Kayla smiled but kept moving. "Come on. Beam's next," she urged.

We hurried across the platform together.

I knew the beam was going to be a pretty easy one for me. Before I moved to California I used to be very involved in gymnastics. That was before I hurt my knee in a vault on the horse. I'm okay now, but I'll never be able to go back to serious gymnastics training. Back then, the beam was my strongest event. After the tough routines filled with jumps, flips, and turns my coach in New York used to put me through, just *walking* across a beam was going to be a piece of cake.

I hurried across the beam without a second thought and then turned to wait for Kayla, who was still on the other platform. She closed her eyes for a moment and bowed her head just a little. For a minute I thought she might be saying a prayer or something. But then her eyes flickered open, and she stared straight ahead of her.

Now that's concentration, I thought as I watched her walk purposefully and briskly across the beam with her eyes focused straight forward. Concentration was never one of my strong points. Even when I used to compete in gymnastics, I was always having too much fun performing to think about concentrating.

"Sandpile!" I called out as we headed to the edge of the platform.

Even though Kayla and I had totally different styles, I could tell that together we were making good time. I jumped down into the sandpile beside her, careful not to put too much pressure on my weaker knee, and we sprinted to the climbing wall. When I saw the dry dirt at the base of the wall, I had an idea. I scooped some up and rubbed it on my hands.

Kayla stared at me.

"Keeps your hands from getting sweaty," I explained quickly. "So you won't lose your grip. We used to do it in gymnastics, but with chalk."

Her face lit up, and she nodded. "I get it. Good idea." She covered her hands with dirt. We both grabbed our ropes, and as we started climbing, Kayla suddenly let out a strange yell. "Eeeeeow!"

Now it was my turn to stare at her.

"It's called a *kiai*," she explained, still pulling on her rope. "It helps center your power. We do it in karate."

"Cool," I said, impressed. I decided to give it a try. "Eeeeeeee-oooow-eee-ooow!" I yelled, pulling on my rope. *Well, I can't say for sure whether that helped me center my power,* I thought, *but it was definitely fun.* I did it again. "Eeeeeeee-oooow-eee-ooow!" I grinned at Kayla, but she was totally focused on what she was doing.

Together we reached the top of the wall. I wiped my dirty hands on my black bicycle shorts, and Kayla and I ran down the ramp.

Kayla looked at me. "Backcountry to park headquarters, right?" she said breathlessly. "It's faster."

I shrugged. "Okay with me. I've never even been in this park before."

"You're kidding," Kayla said, stopping in her tracks.

"No, actually, for once I'm not," I answered. "I just moved here from New York."

"Well, I'm not exactly an expert on the park, but I think I know where I'm going," Kayla responded.

Together we looked at the compass that was hanging around my neck.

"Come on," Kayla said, pulling me toward the woods. "Let's go this way."

A little while later, Kayla and I raced across an open field toward the park headquarters.

"Well, we swung a little too far to the west, so we didn't take the most direct route, but I think we did okay." Kayla was breathing hard between her words.

"Hey, I wouldn't know the difference anyway," I reminded her. "I'm just thankful you got us here."

In the distance, I thought I could see one of the rangers waiting behind the park headquarters building by a tree, watching our progress with binoculars.

I waved, but surprisingly the ranger didn't wave back.

"Who is that?" Kayla asked.

"I thought it was a ranger," I answered. But now that

we were a little closer, I saw that the person wasn't wearing a green and gray ranger uniform after all. I squinted, but the person's face was in shadow. A moment later, whoever it was hurried off between the trees and disappeared.

"That was strange," Kayla commented as we approached the building.

I shrugged. "Maybe it was a bird-watcher or something." I laughed. "Must have been after a pretty important bird, judging by the way whoever it was ran off like that."

Ranger Abe was waiting outside the side entrance to the headquarters building. He smiled at us as we approached.

He glanced at his stopwatch. "Very nice time, girls. Now, just tell me your names."

"Becca Fisher," I answered, still panting from the run.

"Kayla Adams," Kayla managed.

"You did very well," Ranger Abe said again, making a note on his clipboard. "Most important, you showed up here the same way you started out."

"What do you mean?" Kayla asked.

"Yeah, how else would we have showed up, missing an arm or something?" I cracked.

Ranger Abe's gray-blue eyes twinkled. "No, but you might have been missing each other. Sticking together through the obstacle course is important."

"Cool," I said. "Do we get extra points for that?"

He smiled again. "I think you'll find your good teamwork will boost your score quite a bit. Why don't you go on around front, girls, and wait with the others. As soon as everyone's back from the course we'll add up the results and make the announcements."

As we headed for the front of the building, Kayla turned to me. "You know, it never occurred to me to split up. I figured we were in it together to the end."

"*Especially* at the end," I joked. "If we'd split up then I would have been totally lost."

"We never would have gotten here this fast if you hadn't read the compass while I figured out our route," Kayla noted.

"Yeah, I guess working together got us more than just extra points," I replied.

"I think it's really great that they're rewarding people for stuff like teamwork and not littering," Kayla said firmly. "Doing right by the park should be what rangering's all about, if you ask me."

We rounded the corner of the building. About fifteen girls were sitting and lying in the grass in front of park headquarters.

Kayla nodded toward a girl with wavy, shoulder-length light brown hair, who was sitting in the grass reading a magazine. "That's Alex. She's in my class at school. Let's go say hi."

We crossed the grass together.

"What school do you go to, anyway?" I asked Kayla.

"Harmon," she answered. "Harmon Academy. It's a girls' school."

"I didn't think you went to my school," I commented. "Hey, do the girls at Harmon wear those uniforms with the blue skirts? I think I've seen them in town."

Kayla nodded. "We have a choice, actually. Blue skirt, plaid skirt, gray skirt, or gray pants."

"Pants sounds good to me," I said. I almost always wear pants or shorts. That way I can do a handstand or a cartwheel anytime I want without worrying that my dress is going to fly up.

Kayla shook her head. "The pants are wool. The founder of Harmon wanted to make it just like the girls' school she went to back in Boston. Same uniforms and everything. Trouble is, we don't have the same weather here they have in Boston. The blue skirts are the lightest material. That's why everyone wears them."

Kayla's story made me think of all the winter clothes I'd given to my friends back in New York before I'd moved here. As far as I was concerned, one of the definite pluses about moving to California was never having to wear gloves and a scarf again.

Kayla's friend Alex looked up as we approached. "Hi."

"Hi, Alex, this is Becca." Kayla turned to me. "Or is it Rebecca?"

"Definitely Becca," I told her. Actually my real name is Rebecca but absolutely nobody ever calls me that. I make sure of it. I like Becca a lot better.

Kayla and I sat down in the grass.

"Hi," I said to Alex. "So, you go to Kayla's school, huh? What's that you're reading?"

"Hi, yes, *Mountain Bike*," Alex answered.

"Huh?" I said.

Alex smiled, and the corners of her big, brown eyes wrinkled. "Hi, yes I go to Kayla's school, and I'm reading

Mountain Bike magazine." She flipped the magazine over to show me the cover, which featured an action photo of a biker skidding through a mud puddle.

"She was just answering each of your questions, Becca." Kayla laughed. "Alex is extremely logical."

"Oh," I said, understanding at last. "Okay." I grinned. "For a minute I thought you were calling *me* a mountain bike."

We all laughed.

"Do you bike here in the park?" I asked Alex.

She nodded. "Sometimes. Or up by the Heights, where I live."

"The Heights?" I repeated.

"Cayenga Heights," Kayla explained. "It's on the other side of the park. Becca just moved here," she told Alex.

"Where from?" Alex asked.

"New York," I answered. "That's one of the reasons I want to be a junior ranger." I grinned. "I figured it would be a cool way to get to know the new neighborhood."

"The park *is* kind of like a neighborhood for people who live in Cayenga," Kayla agreed. "But people come from all over the country to visit here, too."

"I wish I'd had a chance to get to know the place a little before I had to take that park-knowledge test," I said. "I mean, I studied some maps and stuff at home last night, but there were a bunch of questions I didn't know."

"Well, if you did well on the other tests you may not have to worry," Alex pointed out. "After all, chances are strong that no one girl is going to score at the top in every single subtest. Scoring below average in one area but above average in the other five will still give you an above-average score overall. And then when you factor in the wild cards, the surprise scoring elements, like who held on to their orange tickets after the race, and which girls kept their partners for the obstacle course—"

"Whoa!" I said. "I feel like my brain is overloading!" I laughed. "I see what you mean by logical," I said to Kayla.

"Yeah, Alex is like a human computer," Kayla teased. "That's why they put her in a senior math class even though we're only in ninth grade."

Alex shrugged. She smiled. "I guess what I was trying to say was 'Anything can happen.'"

Kayla shook her head. "If you ask me, everything that happens is *meant* to happen," she said. "I totally believe in karma."

"Karma?" I repeated.

"Sure," Kayla said. "It's an Indian idea. It means that whatever you put out into the world comes back to you in the end. Like if you treat people well and try to do the right thing, then good things will happen to you, too. But if you do stuff you know is wrong, like lie or steal, then someday someone will lie to you or steal from you, too."

"I get it," I said, nodding. I had no idea if Kayla was right, but it definitely seemed like an interesting idea. "Is your family from India?" I asked her. With her pale brown skin, dark hair, and almond-shaped eyes, Kayla seemed like she might have some Indian heritage.

Kayla shook her head. "I'm a bunch of stuff, actually," she explained. "My mom's family is Mexican-American,

Native American, and African-American. My dad's mostly African-American, but he has some Chinese-American in him, too."

"Kayla's a totally American melting-pot girl," Alex commented with a smile.

Just then Ranger Abe joined the group and blew his whistle for attention. Standing beside him were Ranger Lord and Ranger Loukowsky, the two rangers who had given us the test.

"I have the results here," Ranger Abe said, holding up his clipboard, "and I'll get to them in just a moment. First I want to thank each and every one of you for the good work you've done today. This was not an easy test, and you all should be proud of yourselves." He chuckled. "You're a tough group."

Then Ranger Abe looked serious. "But as you know, our exam today was designed to look for some very special qualities, qualities that we feel help to make the best junior rangers. One of the main things—I would say the most important thing—we're looking for is a sense of teamwork. Working in the park, the junior rangers will have to be able to count on one another completely." He paused. "Which is why only those pairs who stayed together for the entire obstacle course will receive scores for that part of the test."

The crowd of girls on the grass burst out at this news. There were cheers and grumbles from all around me. I saw Kayla nodding quietly to herself. I glanced at Alex. *You don't have to be a human computer to see that this is going to shift around the scores a lot,* I said to myself.

"Wow," Alex commented, "talk about a wild card! I'm glad my partner and I stuck it out for that one."

Kayla and I exchanged smiles. Across the lawn, I saw Carson McDonald, the girl jock-star of Cayenga High, and her partner, a red-haired girl I didn't really know, give each other a high five.

"And now I'd like to read the names of the five girls whose overall scores on the test were above passing," Ranger Abe went on.

I felt my palms get sweaty. *Only five people made it?* I thought incredulously. I tried to figure out what the chances were that I might be one of them. I'd scored pretty well on most of the physical tests, although I definitely could have done better on that quiz about the park. Still, I knew I'd gotten extra points for holding on to my orange ticket and staying with my partner.

I really hope I made it, I thought. *Being a junior ranger sounds so cool, not like anything I ever did in New York. And it would be a great way to stay in good physical condition now that I'm not training in gymnastics anymore.* I crossed my fingers for good luck.

Ranger Abe cleared his throat. The crowd of girls grew quiet and waited.

"The first five members of the new girls' division of the Ranger Unit Learning Extension are as follows." He looked down at his clipboard. "Carson McDonald, Sophie Schultz, Kayla Adams, Alex Loomis-Drake, and Rebecca Fisher."

I made it!

"We did it!" Kayla yelled.

Kayla and Alex and I all stood up and high-fived each other. Then, before I even realized what I was doing I jumped up and flipped into a back handspring. *I made it! I made it!*

As I landed on my feet, I saw Ranger Abe looking at me quizzically.

"Oh, by the way, Ranger Abe," I called to him, "there must be some kind of mistake in your records."

"Oh really?" He looked confused.

"Yeah," I said with a grin. "The name's *Becca,* Becca Fisher."

NINE

Later that day, I stood in front of the Cayenga Grill restaurant and studied the SPECIALS board.

CAYENGA GRILL—SATURDAY

SOUP:
Potato Leek

SPECIAL APPETIZERS:
Mixed Baby Greens with Goat Cheese
Shrimp Tostada

DINNER SPECIALS:
Wild Mushroom Ravioli with Broccoli
Halibut with Lemon Pepper Crust

DESSERTS:
Homemade Cinnamon Ice Cream
Strawberry Cheese Tart

I stood back and fidgeted with the piece of chalk in my hand. *Too boring,* I thought, reading the menu I had written out. *It needs something else.*

I squatted down in front of the board. Right beside the listing for "Strawberry Cheese Tart" I added the words:

Berry, berry delicious!!!

There, I thought. *That's better. And it's true, too. Barry's strawberry cheese tart is incredibly good. He and Mom can't get mad at me for adding that to the board,* I reasoned. *Not like they did a couple of weeks ago when I added something extra to the listing for "Chocolate Mud Pie."* I still didn't really see what the big deal was that time, though. The whole thing was supposed to be a joke. I didn't think any of the customers would actually *believe* it when I wrote "Made with real mud!"

Still, my stepfather and my mother didn't think it was so funny. Barry explained to me that the first few weeks a restaurant is open are really important. He said this was the Cayenga Grill's chance to make a name for itself. And I guess I understand. Barry and my mom put everything they had into opening this restaurant. Back in New York, they worked in someone else's restaurant. Barry was a cook, and my mom was the manager. I know it means a lot to both of them to actually *own* a restaurant at last.

I walked back inside and put the chalk away behind the hosts' stand. The restaurant was empty now. All the lunch customers were gone, and it wasn't time for the dinner crowd yet. Mo, the older man who helps us out busing tables and working as a janitor, was silently sweeping in the corner.

"Hi, Mo," I said in a friendly voice. "How's it going?"

Mo turned slowly to face me. He didn't say anything, just nodded. Then he went back to sweeping. Mo doesn't talk much.

"Hey, Mo," I called after him. "Seen any good movies lately?"

Mo didn't even stop sweeping, just shook his head.

"Okay, well, catch you later," I said, cheerfully. For some reason it drives me crazy that Mo's always so silent and serious. I guess you could say I'm on a mission. I just know that one of these days I'll get him to crack a smile.

I walked back to the kitchen and found my stepfather, Barry, carefully placing strawberries on the tarts. His white chef's apron was wrapped around him, and he had smears of flour on his face.

"Hi, Becca," he said. "You finish writing the specials out front?"

"Yeah." Barry knows I love writing the specials on the board, so he saves it for me if he knows I'm coming to the restaurant that day. That's the kind of person Barry is. I guess I'm pretty lucky to have him for a stepfather. My own dad died when I was just a baby. I never even knew him, really. My mom's been married to Barry since I was six. He's the only real father I've ever known.

I watched as Barry poured some red glaze over the strawberries. "Hey, Barry, did I tell you about how my partner, Kayla, and I climbed up the wall today in the test?" I asked. "We put dirt on our hands and—"

"Only about three times already," Barry said with a smile.

"Oh," I replied, disappointed. "I guess I'm kind of excited that I passed," I added. I picked up a strawberry from the counter and popped it in my mouth.

"I think it's great, too," Barry agreed. "When do you start?"

"Tomorrow," I answered. "There's a big meeting of both divisions, boys' and girls', at one o'clock."

"I guess that means I'm going to lose my extra brunch waitress tomorrow," Barry commented.

"Oh, that's right!" I said, remembering. I often help out at the restaurant during busy times. The past two weeks I'd done some waitressing during the Sunday brunch shift. "Are you going to be okay without me?"

"Well, I don't know," Barry began. "Now that you're a certified junior park ranger, we might need you around here more than ever."

I laughed. "How's that?"

"Well, what if we have an emergency?" Barry went on. "What if a couple of customers get lost on the trail to the rest rooms or something?"

I laughed again. "Oh, right. Or what if there's a whipped cream avalanche?"

"Or a chocolate mud pie mud slide!" Barry added.

Just then my mother walked in the room with my eight-year-old half brother, Simon.

"Happy cooks in the kitchen, that's what I like to see," my mother said with a smile.

Mmmmm! Strawberry tarts, that's what I like to see!" Simon added.

We all laughed.

"I was just telling Becca how valuable it was going to be to have a real junior ranger working with us here at the restaurant," Barry said to my mother.

An expression of concern crossed my mother's face. "Actually, Becca, I need to talk to you about that. You may not be able to do this ranger thing after all."

I stared at her. "Mom! What are you talking about? Of course I'm going to do it!"

"Becca, a ranger called the house this afternoon, just after you left to come here," my mother told me. "He said he was calling to warn you about an outbreak of rabies at the park."

"Rabies?" I said incredulously. "Are you sure?"

"What's rabies?" Simon asked.

"That doesn't make any sense," I said. *After all,* I reasoned, *if there was some kind of problem at the park, wouldn't Ranger Abe have told us about it that morning at the test?* "Who was this guy?"

"He said his name was Ranger John," my mother replied. "And he seemed to think you might be in danger if you go to work in the park."

"But I was just at the park this morning, and no one said anything about a rabies outbreak!" I objected.

"What's rabies?" Simon asked again. "Can I have a strawberry tart?"

"Rabies is a dangerous disease that's carried by animals," Barry explained. "If an animal with rabies bites you then you can get the disease. If it's not treated right away, there's no cure for it. And no, you can't have a tart until after dinner."

"Aw, that's not fair!" Simon complained.

"Becca, I don't want you going to that park if it means putting yourself in danger," my mother said.

"This whole thing is ridiculous," I said. "I was just at the park this morning, and everything was fine. How could there suddenly be an outbreak of rabies? I'm calling the park to find out what's going on." I walked across the kitchen and picked up the phone.

"That's probably a good idea," my mother said. She turned to my brother. "Simon, get your fingers away from that tart! Tell you what. Becca, you call the park. Simon, why don't you and I leave Barry and those tarts alone for a while. Let's go out back and play a quick game of catch before I have to get the dining room ready for dinner. Becca, let me know what you find out!"

As my mom and Simon left the room I dialed directory assistance and got the main number for Cayenga Park. After a couple of rings, a recorded announcement began listing the park's hours and other information. There was no mention of any kind of rabies bulletin, so I held on for an operator.

A moment later a man answered the phone. "Cayenga Park ranger station. Ranger O'Rourke speaking."

"Yes, hi," I said. "I heard there was some kind of rabies alert in the park, and I was wondering if I could get some more information. I'm one of the new junior rangers, and I need to know if I'm still supposed to come to the park tomorrow."

Barry stopped working and moved closer to listen.

"Rabies alert?" the ranger repeated. "Oh, no, I'm afraid you must be mistaken."

"But a ranger called my house today," I explained. "He said there had been an outbreak of rabies in the park," I added.

"Hold on a minute and I'll double-check with park headquarters," the ranger said.

I waited while he put me on hold. "He's checking," I told Barry.

A couple of minutes later the ranger came back on the line. "I don't know who called you and gave you that information, or why, but there's definitely no rabies alert."

"So everything's okay?" I asked. "The park's open and the junior rangers are still supposed to show up for our meeting tomorrow?"

"That's correct," the ranger assured me.

"Okay, thanks," I replied. I hung up and turned to Barry. "He said there's no rabies alert at all. He said we must be mistaken."

"But what about that man who called your mother?" Barry asked.

"The ranger I just talked to said he had no idea why somebody would call and tell us something like that," I responded with a shrug. "But he guaranteed me that everything's okay at the park. Hey, maybe it was a wrong number or something. Or maybe it was somebody's idea of a joke."

Somebody with a really bad sense of humor, I added silently.

TEN

The following morning I rode with my mom and Barry to the restaurant to help set up for brunch and wait some tables until it was time to go to the park. Luckily, Simon was playing at a friend's house that morning, so he didn't have to come with us. Simon always complains when he has to hang around the restaurant. I guess I don't blame him. It's more fun for me, since I get to help out and talk to the customers and stuff. Poor Simon spends most of his time tossing his baseball against the wall out back or playing with his Super Charger Mega Fighter video game upstairs in the storeroom. I guess he gets kind of bored and lonely.

Around twenty minutes to one I said good-bye to my mom and Barry and headed to the park. The Cayenga Grill is on the southern edge of town, so it's not too far from the park. In fact, since the restaurant is up on a little hill, there's even a view of the park from the dining room's south windows. I figured I'd be able to make it on foot to park headquarters for the meeting in twenty minutes or less.

I entered the park through the main entrance. The ranger in the booth at the parking lot wasn't anyone I knew, but I waved to her anyway, and she waved back. *You don't know me yet, but starting today we're working together,* I thought with pride as I walked past the booth and into the park.

As I headed up the path to headquarters, I heard a voice behind me.

"Hey, um, I mean . . . hello!"

I turned and saw the red-haired girl who had been Carson McDonald's partner in the obstacle course the day before. She was dressed in a bright pink and purple flowered T-shirt and patched jeans, and her long red hair was pulled into a ponytail.

"Oh, hi. You're Sophie, right?" I said, remembering.

She jogged to catch up with me. "That's right. Are you . . . Alex?" she guessed.

I shook my head. "I'm Becca. Alex is the one with a built-in keyboard," I joked.

"Huh?" Sophie looked at me, confused.

"Nothing." I laughed. "Just a joke. I met Alex yesterday. She's really smart. They call her the human computer."

"Oh." Now Sophie laughed, too. Then she rolled her eyes. "I'd hate to tell you what *my* nickname is."

"Go on," I said. "I'll tell you mine."

"Well, okay." Sophie's cheeks reddened a little. "It's

'Soppy.' At least, that's what my brother, Jason, calls me. I hate it."

"Wow, if my brother ever called me anything like that I'd probably string him up by his toenails," I commented.

"Yeah, well, how old is your brother?" Sophie asked.

"Eight."

"Jason's fifteen," she told me. "At least, he's fifteen on the outside. Inside he's about three and a half."

We both laughed.

"So what *is* your nickname, anyway, Becca?" she asked me.

I shrugged. "Becca," I answered.

Sophie burst out laughing.

I grinned. *I like this girl already,* I decided, pulling open the door to the park headquarters building. *Working with her is definitely going to be fun.*

When we got inside, there were already about ten kids scattered around the main meeting room on folding chairs. At first I saw only boys, but then I spotted Carson sitting on the far side of the room. She was talking to a slim African-American guy with a green baseball cap perched backward on his head. Carson waved when she saw us, and we headed over.

"Hi, you guys," Carson said. "This is Walker. He's on the swim team with my brother Logan. He's also in the boys' division. Walker, this is Sophie and Becca."

Walker smiled. "Nice to meet you. Welcome to the junior rangers."

"Thanks," I said. I glanced around the room. "There sure are a lot of guys here."

"Well, the boys' junior division *has* been around for ten years," Walker pointed out.

"That must make for some pretty old 'juniors,'" I joked.

Walker laughed. "Of course none of *us* has actually been here that long. Although there are quite a few rangers working in the park who started out as juniors."

Just then, Kayla walked into the room. I waved to her. She waved back and headed over to where we were sitting.

"Hi, everybody." Kayla pulled up a chair and sat down, folding her legs up under her long brown and yellow flowered sundress. She turned to Walker, Carson, and Sophie. "I'm Kayla."

"Hi, Kayla," Sophie and Carson said together.

"Hi, I'm Walker," Walker volunteered, turning toward Kayla. As he turned his head, I noticed that his baseball cap was printed with the words CAYENGA PARK.

"Hey, Walker, I like your cap," I said. "Do we get those, too?"

He shrugged. "Probably. Everyone in the Learning Extension gets park caps, T-shirts, and windbreakers."

"Oh, great," Kayla moaned. "Not another uniform!"

"It's not actually a uniform," Walker explained. "The caps and the T-shirts and stuff are all voluntary—you only wear them when you want to. The only thing you always have to have on is your badge." He tilted his torso a little to show us the small rectangular plastic badge pinned to his white T-shirt.

CALIFORNIA STATE PARKS
CAYENGA COUNTY REGION
CAYENGA PARK

Ranger Unit Learning Extension

Walker Young

"Okay, I think I can handle that," Kayla said with a smile.

"Kayla wears a uniform to school," I explained to the others.

"I spend my life in uniforms!" Kayla counted off on her fingers. "One uniform for school, another one for karate—"

Walker cut her off. "You do karate? Really?"

Kayla nodded. "My dad has a dojo over on Mission Drive."

"What's a dojo?" Sophie asked.

"In Japanese it means 'way place,' or 'place of learning,'" Kayla explained. "It's a school or a studio for studying martial arts."

"It's also the name of a really great Japanese restaurant near my old apartment in New York," I put in.

Everyone laughed.

"Are you really from New York?" Sophie asked me, her eyes wide.

I nodded.

"That's so cool," Sophie said. "I've always wanted to go to New York."

I smiled. I think it's so funny when people are impressed that I come from New York. After all, to me New York is just my old hometown.

Just then, the door opened, and a middle-aged man with thinning brown hair and a tall, muscular frame hurried into the room. At first I thought he might be there to help lead the meeting, but then I realized that he wasn't wearing a ranger's uniform. The man glanced at the group quickly and then hurried through the room to a door at the far left marked OFFICE.

Two other guys who were sitting on chairs nearby turned to face us. One of them had dark, wavy, longish hair, and the other one had a short, brown buzz-cut.

"Excuse me, did you just say your dad owns the martial arts place on Mission?" the one with the long hair asked Kayla.

Kayla nodded enthusiastically. "Do you know it?"

"I live near there," he replied. "I was thinking of taking some classes."

"You should stop by sometime," Kayla urged. "My dad offers a free trial class if you're interested."

Suddenly the conversation was interrupted by yelling from the right side of the room.

"Soppy! Oh, Soppy!"

I turned and saw a guy with red hair and freckles just like Sophie's. He had just come in, along with another, taller boy with very dark hair. The two boys were elbowing each other and cracking up, practically doubling over with laughter.

"Hi, Soppy!" the red-haired boy yelled again.

"Let me guess," I said to Sophie. "That's Jason."

Two bright pink spots had appeared on Sophie's cheeks. "I can't stand it when he does this," she said between clenched teeth.

"Hey, Walker!" the boy beside Jason yelled out. "Looks like you're on the wrong side of the room! You belong over here with us, not with the Girl Scouts!"

A few of the boys laughed.

"Aw, come on, Rick, give them a break," Walker said gently.

I'd like to give them a break, I thought. *I'd like to break something right over both of their heads! These guys definitely need a little taste of their own medicine,* I decided. I stood up and walked toward them with a big smile on my face.

"Hi, there," I said in my best fake-cheerful voice. "I'm Becca, one of the new junior rangers." I stuck my hand out toward Sophie's brother. "I guess you must be *Jerk*son."

Jason stared at me, his eyes popping with surprise. A few of the guys in the room snickered.

"Ha-ha, Jason, she got you there!" Rick cried.

Jason narrowed his eyes. "Very funny."

"*I* thought it was," Sophie said from her seat behind me. I turned to look at her. She had a huge smile on her face.

"Why don't you and your friends just go home and give it up," Rick said to Sophie. "Everyone knows this whole idea to let girls in the junior rangers is really stupid."

"Yeah, well, I guess you're the expert," I said to him.

"That's right." Rick folded is arms over his chest and looked pleased with himself. "I've been a junior ranger for two years."

"Oh, no, I meant you're the expert on *stupid*," I corrected him.

There was more laughter in the room, but I also heard some boys rooting out loud for Rick.

Carson spoke up next. "What's stupid is fighting about it like this. Don't you realize we're all here for the same reason, because we want to help the park?"

"That's right," Kayla added. "Besides, we all passed the exact same test you did to get in here. We have just as much right to be junior rangers as you do."

"I'd watch out for her if I were you, Rick," the boy sitting near us with the buzz-cut remarked, nodding toward Kayla. "She knows karate."

"Oh, are you a black belt or something?" Rick asked Kayla with a sneer.

"Not yet," Kayla replied coolly. "But I am a purple belt. That's the fourth degree up in our type of karate. I've been taking classes with my dad since I was five."

"Uh-oh, I better be careful," Rick said mockingly. "She might beat me up or something." Jason was snickering beside him.

What a jerk, I thought. I turned to look at Kayla. *If someone made a crack like that about me I'd be really angry.*

But Kayla's face was stony as she regarded Rick. The only hint that she might be upset was in her deep rust-brown eyes, which were focused directly and intensely on him.

Rick's laughter died out under Kayla's stare. The room grew silent.

"Students of karate spend a lot of time practicing self-control," Kayla said at last, her voice even. "We have to. After all, we're training our bodies to become lethal weapons. So you don't have to be worried, Rick." She smiled just a little. "I only use *my* weapon when I have to."

What a cool girl! I thought admiringly. *Nothing seems to rattle her at all!*

Rick's mouth was open, but no sound was coming out. He looked like he was trying to think of something to say. Everyone else was silent, waiting.

Just at that moment the door opened, and Ranger Abe walked into the room.

"Well, hello there, folks," he boomed cheerfully. "I see everybody's getting to know our newest members."

"Oh, sure," I mumbled. "It's a regular get-acquainted party in here."

Alex came rushing in the door behind Ranger Abe. She was dressed in black leggings and a black tank top, and she was wearing a black bicycle helmet. In her hands was a bicycle wheel.

"Hi," she said breathlessly. "Sorry I'm late. Did I miss anything?"

"No, no, we're just getting started," Ranger Abe assured her. "Why don't you all find seats so we can begin."

I waved to Alex, and she brought over a chair and sat down between me and Kayla. Sophie and Carson, who were directly in front of us, turned and waved to her.

"You're Alex, right?" Sophie asked.

Alex nodded.

"I'm Sophie, and this is Carson."

Alex nodded. "Hi." She took off her bicycle helmet and leaned her bike wheel against her chair.

"Did you have a problem with your bike?" I asked her, looking down at the wheel.

She followed my gaze. "Oh, this?" She held the wheel up again for a moment. "No, it's supposed to come off. I built the bike with a quick-release front wheel so I could take it off easily when I go indoors. That way I don't have to worry about anyone stealing my bike."

"You *built* your own bike?" I asked her incredulously.

She nodded. "Last year. I'm building a motorbike now."

"Wow." I was impressed. "I've never built anything in my life," I said. "Well, maybe a tower or something out of blocks when I was about five, but nothing since then."

Alex smiled. "I'm really into mechanical stuff. When I get the motorbike finished you can take it out for a ride sometime," she offered.

"Thanks," I said. "That sounds cool."

Ranger Abe had taken his place in the front of the room and was calling for everyone's attention. The room grew silent.

"First of all, I want to welcome our newest members to the Learning Extension, our charter members of the girls' division. They are Sophie Schultz, Carson McDonald, Kayla Adams, Alex Loomis-Drake, and *Becca* Fisher." He paused to smile at me. "Welcome to the park, girls. I'm going to talk a little bit about what some of your responsibilities will be, and then I'll discuss the special training you'll be getting in CPR and water safety. I'll also be handing out your Ranger Unit Learning Extension badges, as well as some Cayenga Park T-shirts, baseball hats, and jackets. Oh, and I'm afraid I'm going to need you to fill out some information forms again with your names and addresses and phone numbers. Somehow the ones you filled out at the test yesterday seem to have been misplaced."

Out of the corner of my eye, I saw Rick raise his hand.

"Yes, Rick?" Ranger Abe responded.

"I was just wondering, do us guys have to sit here while you talk to the girls about all this beginner stuff?" Rick asked. "I mean, we all already know all this, and we have our certifications and everything. Can't we just go out to the park?"

Ranger Abe's expression grew stern. "Let me remind you, Rick, that there was a time that you were new to the Learning Extension, too. And I'm sure the veteran members were patient with you while you learned what you needed to know."

Rick slumped in his seat, his arms folded across his chest.

I raised my hand.

"Yes, Becca?" Ranger Abe nodded to me.

"I just wanted to let you know that I'm *already*

certified in CPR." I shot Rick a glance. "I took it last spring at my old school."

"Wonderful," Ranger Abe replied. "Just bring me a copy of your certification."

For the next ten minutes, Ranger Abe described when and where the water safety and CPR classes would be held, and told us a little bit about what our duties would be in the park. He explained that many of the jobs, like lifeguarding, leading hikes, and working the information booth by the campgrounds, would be rotated among us. In addition, we'd all be expected to patrol the park on foot and by bike.

Ranger Abe went on. "Now that we have five extra junior rangers in the park, we'll also be able to think of ways to expand the program a bit. The new supervisor, Ms. Rodriguez, and I are meeting soon to discuss some ideas she has about how to best use our new manpower— oops, make that *person*-power." Ranger Abe smiled. "For instance, I believe Ms. Rodriguez wants to start some educational programs for kids from the area grade schools to help them learn about the park."

"Good idea. The girls can work with the little kids while the guys do the *real* ranger stuff," Rick commented.

A few of the boys laughed.

"I'm sure the education program would be worked into the rotation of regular jobs, so everyone would have a chance to be a part of it," Ranger Abe said pointedly.

Just then the door on the left marked OFFICE opened, and the man I'd seen earlier came out.

Ranger Abe seemed surprised to see him. "Oh, hello, Dr. Burr. Did you need some help with something?"

Dr. Burr seemed taken by surprise as well. "Oh, no, no. I was just in the office to borrow a screwdriver from the toolbox." He patted the pocket of his shirt.

"Again? That's the second time in two days. Dr. Burr, you sure do seem to be having some repair problems up there in that study center. What is it this time? Something I can have one of the rangers help you with?" Ranger Abe asked good-naturedly.

Dr. Burr shook his head. "Just the old screen door again. I can take care of it on my own." He hurried in the direction of the exit door.

"Oh, wait, before you go I want to introduce you to our newest rangers, in the girls' division," Ranger Abe called. "Everybody, this is Dr. Lyle Burr. Dr. Burr is a research scientist who has been working in the park on a series of special wildlife projects for the past ten years. Dr. Burr works and lives at a special study center in the woods up beyond the public campground."

Dr. Burr turned to face us for the first time, and suddenly his manner seemed to change. A moment ago he had appeared to be in a big hurry, but now he greeted us with a smile and a wave.

"Well, hello there, girls!" he said brightly. "Welcome to you all! I can't tell you how happy I am that the park has finally set up an extension division for girls. Really, I'm so pleased! But it's a tough job, you know! So, good luck to you all. Now, if you'll excuse me, I'll just take my wrench and be off." He patted the pocket of his shirt again and hurried out the door.

Ranger Abe turned back to the group. "Now, there was one more important thing I wanted to talk to you all about today, something I want you all to be on the lookout for as you patrol the park. We're having a bit of a problem with illegal hunting. As you all probably know, there's no hunting or trapping of any kind allowed in the park. A few months back we had some trouble, but I thought we'd taken care of it. However, yesterday at the end of our qualifying test a couple of our new junior rangers informed me that they'd spotted a leghold trap by the river."

A murmur went through the room.

I turned to Alex. "Who saw the trap?" I whispered. "Do you know?"

"It must have been Carson and Sophie," she answered.

"How do you know?" I asked.

"Process of elimination," she replied. "There are only five of us who are new rangers, right? So I know it wasn't you or me, and if it were Kayla she would have mentioned something after the test yesterday. The only two left are Carson and Sophie."

"Oh," I said. *Why didn't I think of that? It sounds so simple when she puts it that way,* I thought.

"I sent some rangers to check the area, but the trap had been removed," Ranger Abe went on. "In any case, I want all of you to be on the lookout for signs of illegal hunting in the area over the next few days."

"Don't worry about it, Ranger Abe, we'll take care of it!" a boy called out.

"Yeah, with us guys in the park, those poachers are toast," Rick boasted.

"Mmmm, poachers and toast. Sounds like a breakfast special," I joked.

A bunch of people laughed.

Ranger Abe put up his hand. "I also want to caution you to be extremely careful. Illegal hunters, or poachers, can be dangerous, and they're often armed. Be sure to report any suspicious behavior as well as any evidence of traps or guns to a ranger at once."

I felt a chill go up my spine. *Nothing like this ever happened in New York!* I thought with excitement. I imagined myself nabbing a poacher in the act and turning him in.

"All right then, we're just about finished with the meeting," Ranger Abe said. "I'll conclude by telling the girls' division about a special assignment I have for them."

I sat up straighter and listened. *Our first assignment! It sounds so official,* I thought happily. I was definitely loving this junior ranger stuff already.

"No fair!" Jason burst out. "Why do they get a special assignment?"

"Yeah," another boy echoed. "What about us?"

Ranger Abe put his hand up. "This is an assignment that is designed to help the new girls' division to bond as a unit. In fact, the boys' division did it, too, back when it was first formed ten years ago, and it did wonders for the group's team spirit. It's an overnight survival camping trip on one of the park's highest mountains, Mesa del Oro. I think making it through a night on the mountain together with only the barest provisions will be an excellent way for you girls to bond as a team."

"You mean an excellent way for them to bond as a bunch of chickens," Rick muttered.

A few of the boys began to snicker. Someone clucked like a chicken.

"What was that comment, Rick?" Ranger Abe demanded.

"I just don't think the girls can do it, that's all," Rick said. "I don't think they'll make it through the first hour after dark on that mountain alone."

"My sister won't, that's for sure," Jason added.

"Be quiet, Jason!" Sophie responded.

"You be quiet!" Jason shot back.

"*Everyone* be quiet!" Ranger Abe was clearly frustrated. He paused, thinking. A sly smile crept over his lips. "Rick, maybe you have a point. Maybe the girls shouldn't be out there alone on the mountain."

Kayla stood up. "Excuse me, Ranger Abe, but we can do it. I know we can."

Ranger Abe smiled. "I know you can do it, too. You're tough kids. You made it through the qualifying test, and you're going to make great junior rangers. What I meant was, maybe the girls shouldn't be the only ones who have to camp out on the mountain. After all, none of you boys were here when your unit did its night on the mountain ten years ago. Maybe I should send both groups out for the survival trip."

"Oh, come on," Rick complained. "We don't need a survival trip. We're already a team."

"Even so, I think a night on the mountain will be good for both groups," Ranger Abe declared. "It's settled.

Boys, you'll camp out on the west side of Mesa del Oro, and girls, you'll be on the east side. We'll schedule the trip for next Saturday."

I turned to Alex and Kayla with a grin. "A camping trip on a mountain—how cool! I never did anything like this back in New York!"

ALEX

ELEVEN

Now, where is that thing? I wondered. I stood up on my tiptoes, straining to see the top shelf of my closet. *No good. I'll have to climb up there and look.*

I walked back out into my room and grabbed a chair. It wasn't the sturdiest chair in the world. It had spindly little legs, and the seat was covered with some kind of silky cream-colored upholstery. But it would have to do.

I propped the chair in a corner of the closet and climbed up on it.

Where is that sleeping bag? I wondered again. I tried to remember the last time I had used it. *Think, Alex.* Then I remembered. *Two months ago, the night I slept out in the garden so I could watch the Nolan comet when it passed through our part of the sky.* I always sleep outside when there's going to be a major event in the solar system. And the Nolan comet was definitely a major event. According to the Starwatch website on the Internet, the comet wasn't due to come our way for another 143 years. I was glad I hadn't missed it.

Right now I was looking for my sleeping bag for another reason. I was about to take my first camping trip in Cayenga Park, on Mesa del Oro. I had just made it to the new girls' division of the junior rangers, and our first assignment was a survival trip together on the mountain.

But my sleeping bag was nowhere in sight. I started taking things down from the closet and putting them on the floor. I did find my backpack, which I knew I would need. I also found a bunch of other junk, including a half-deflated basketball, a pair of in-line skates I'd grown out of, and two bicycle pumps. And here was my old mint-green bedspread from before when my parents decided to have my room redecorated in cream and salmon. Next to it was a box full of wires, plugs, and other neat-looking electrical equipment. Behind that was the trophy I got back in third grade for winning the California State Science Competition. But still no sleeping bag.

I held the trophy in my hand, remembering how proud I'd been of the invention I'd entered in that contest. It was a remote-controlled cart on a track for passing salt, sugar, ketchup, and other stuff at the dinner table. I was sure I'd come up with something no family could live without. That was back before I realized that not every family has a big formal dining room like ours with a table about a million miles long.

I tossed my backpack into my room and put the trophy with the other stuff on the floor of my closet. I stepped out and surveyed my room carefully, trying to think of where I might have stashed the sleeping bag. I gazed at the other cream-colored chair, my two pale wood dressers, and my desk and computer. My eyes passed over my shelves full of stereo equipment and books, and my bed with its new salmon-colored spread, and finally came to rest on my window seat.

That's it! I thought, remembering the storage compartment under the window seat. I hurried over and slid open the panel.

The section of the wall where the window seat was built in my room is over the western wing of our house, which faces the pool and the ocean. The west veranda, by the pool, is directly under my room, and its roof juts out from right under my window. I love having my window seat there, because it means I have a view of the cliff and the ocean below from it. It also means that there's a deep, narrow crawl space that leads from my window seat out under the roof below. When I was a little kid I used to like to sit in there in the dark on really hot summer days. Now I use it as a storage area.

I stuck my head and shoulders into the narrow space and felt around. There were a few dust-bunnies, an old cardboard carton—

"Alex?" I heard my mother's voice in the room behind me. "Alex? What are you doing in there?"

As she spoke my hand landed on a familiar stuffed nylon pouch. *That's it! I found it!*

I backed out of the crawl space with the sleeping bag in my hand. My mother was standing in my room looking down at me curiously. I noticed that she was dressed in a deep blue suit and white blouse, even though it was a Saturday.

"Are you going to work?" I asked her.

She shook her head. "I'm taping an interview for the *California Today* show," she explained. "They want to talk to me about the Washburn case."

"Oh," I said. Actually, I couldn't remember what the Washburn case was. You see, my mom's a lawyer, and she handles a lot of well-known cases.

"And you?" She reached out and pulled a dust-bunny out of my hair and smiled. "What are you doing? I thought you stopped hiding under that window seat when you were seven."

I laughed. "I had to get my sleeping bag," I explained. "Today's my big camping trip in the park."

"Camping trip?" My mother raised her eyebrows in surprise.

"Didn't Daddy tell you?" I asked. "I told him all about it last week, right after the junior ranger meeting."

My mother sighed. "No, I guess he forgot. He's been so busy negotiating that big movie deal for Rod Jarvis."

My father is a Hollywood agent. He represents a lot of big stars, like the action-hero actor Rod Jarvis.

"Well, Daddy knows all about it," I said again. I walked over and picked up my backpack. "I'm camping out on Mesa del Oro tonight, in the park. It's a survival trip."

"Survival trip—I'm not sure I like the sound of that," my mother said. "What does that mean exactly?"

I opened the drawer to one of my dressers. "It means we camp out with only a few provisions. It's like a test, us against nature, to see how we survive and to help us feel like a team." I pulled out some long johns and stuffed them into my pack.

My mother looked worried. "I don't think I like this idea, Alex."

"But Mom," I objected, "you said you were behind me a hundred percent when I told you I wanted to work in the park."

"I do support the idea of your volunteering for something, Alex. I believe strongly in volunteering. We are a very fortunate family, and I think it's wonderful that you want to give something back to the community. All I'm saying is why can't you do something a little less . . . adventurous? There's a lawyer in my firm, Ken Dean. He's connected with an organization called Voluntime. Maybe he could set you up with something nice, like tutoring kids or reading out loud to senior citizens once a month."

"Mom, I don't want to read out loud to senior citizens," I said. "I mean, I'm sure it's a great program, but I want to be a junior ranger. I *like* adventure." I put a pair of jeans and a Cayenga Park T-shirt into my pack.

My mother sighed. "I know, and I don't know where you got it from, either. Lisa and Trish never did anything like this."

Lisa and Trish are my two sisters. Lisa's away at college now, and Trish is in seventh grade at Harmon Academy, where I go to school, too.

"Well, Trish considers shopping for shoes to be an adventure," I said scornfully. "But you did let Lisa go on that scuba-diving trip with her friends in Mexico when she was my age. Remember?"

"That was different," my mother insisted. "It was a bunch of girls from her class at Harmon, and they all stayed on the Redfields' family yacht down there. Besides, Mexico was warm. A mountain in the middle of the night is going to be freezing."

"Mom, 'freezing' means thirty-two degrees Fahrenheit," I corrected. "It hasn't hit thirty-two in early October in Cayenga in . . ." I paused. "Hang on, I'll go look it up on my computer."

"No, no, that's all right, Alex." My mother laughed. "I believe you. You'd make a great lawyer, you know that?"

It's a good thing my mother wasn't around when that weird phone call came for me last week, I thought, remembering. Some man had called and left a message for me with Mary, our maid, about some kind of rabies outbreak in the park. I checked the data for rabies in our area on my computer, though, and there hadn't been anything like an outbreak in at least five years. The Cayenga Park website didn't mention anything about a recent problem either. I decided it had to have been a mistake. Or possibly a prank of some kind.

"It's just that I have a hard time understanding why you would *volunteer* to spend a night outside on a cold mountain when you have a perfectly lovely room here," my mother went on. "But I guess we're just different that way."

"I guess so, Mom." I stuffed a sweater into my backpack. "Anyway, I didn't exactly volunteer for the trip. All the junior rangers have to do it. It's required."

"Well, darling, if that's it, why don't you let me make a few phone calls," my mother said. "I'm sure we know someone who has friends in the park. Let's see, I handled that case two years ago for Richard Donner. Why, he donated over a million dollars to the parks department last year! I'll just give him a buzz. I'm sure we can get you excused from the trip."

Now it was my turn to laugh. "Mom, thanks but no thanks," I said. I buckled my pack and slung it over my shoulder. "I *want* to go on this trip. And don't worry, I'll be fine."

TWELVE

Forty-five minutes later, I was coasting on my bike down the steep grade from Cayenga Heights toward the southwest entrance to the park. I love riding my bike. I built it myself last year, but I started researching and shopping for parts in catalogues a full year before that. I wanted to combine the best of everything—the best brakes with the best frame with the best tires. The only way to do that is to make it yourself.

And it was worth all the work, too. My bike rides like a dream. Right now, coasting along the wooded, mountainous road with a cool breeze on my face, my pack on my back, and my sleeping bag tied to the rack on my bike, I felt like I was flying.

I waved to the ranger in the booth at the entrance to the park, and he waved back. The road into the park from the southwest winds through the mountains before heading down to park headquarters. I knew there were some sharp turns and steep hills up ahead, so I got a firm grip on my handlebars and concentrated on the road in front of me.

As the road wound past the vineyards, a couple of cars cruised by me from behind, pulling carefully to the left side of the road as they passed to give me room. The driver of the second car, a green Cayenga Park jeep, tooted the horn lightly in greeting. I waved back.

A little while later the road came out along the side of a mountain, near the base. I could see the sparkling blue of the reservoir just below to my right. I also spotted a pretty steep grade in the road ahead of me. *It's definitely going to take some leg power to make it up that hill,* I realized, *especially with the added weight of my pack and sleeping bag on the bike.*

I took a deep breath and started pedaling strongly but evenly. In the distance ahead of me I could hear the roar of a car's engine. It still sounded pretty far off, but I pulled a little to the right just to be safe.

As I pedaled up the incline, the sound of the car grew much louder. I realized that it was coming my way much more quickly than I had anticipated. But it was too late. Suddenly the car appeared in front of me, careening around the bend in the road at top speed. It seemed to be headed right for me!

"Hey!" I yelled.

I quickly checked the road to my right, but there was barely any shoulder, only a small ditch. And the drop to the reservoir below was at least ten feet. I didn't know what to do.

At the last moment I jerked my handlebars to the right

anyway. It was either that or get hit by the car. My bike skidded in the gravel and slid out from under me, landing me in the ditch.

I shielded my face as the car flew past me, dust and gravel spraying out from under its wheels. The driver was obviously going way above the speed limit. I quickly tried to check the license plate. But the car left a cloud of dust behind it and I couldn't see the plate at all.

I picked myself up and dusted myself off. My knee was scraped, but not too badly. I was more worried about my bike. I picked it up and wheeled it carefully back out onto the road, where I quickly inspected it. Luckily, there didn't seem to be any damage to it, either.

The rest of my ride was a whole lot less fun. My knee was stinging, and I was feeling kind of shaky after what had happened. I was relieved when I saw the park headquarters building up ahead.

As I pedaled into the parking lot, I could see that Kayla and Becca were already there, sitting on the grass together with their backpacks beside them. Kayla goes to my school, but I'd just met Becca a week before, at the tryouts. A couple of yards away, clustered near the entrance to the building, were seven or eight of the guys from the boys' division.

I backed my bike into the bike rack and snapped off the easy-release front wheel. I headed over toward where Kayla and Becca were sitting.

"Hi, Alex," Kayla said.

"Hi." I sat down in the grass beside them.

"Hi, Alex." Becca nudged my bicycle wheel with her

foot. "Well, it looks like you're *wheely* weady for the big twip," she joked.

Kayla groaned. "That one was terrible, Becca." She laughed. "Do you ever stop kidding around?"

Becca nodded. "Certainly. The third Tuesday of every month. I take it off. I don't tell a single joke all day." She grinned. "Just kidding."

We all laughed.

Just then a ranger vehicle pulled into the parking lot. The passenger door opened, and Carson jumped out, backpack in hand.

The blonde woman in a ranger uniform in the front seat of the car waved to Carson, and Carson waved back. The jeep did a quick U-turn, pulled out of the parking lot, and headed down the road.

Carson spotted us and hurried over to where we were sitting.

"Hi, Carson, I'm impressed," Becca said with a smile. "You've only been a junior ranger for a few days and you're already getting rides around the park in jeeps."

Carson laughed. "Oh, that was just my mom," she said.

"Your mom?" I repeated in surprise. "Your mother is a ranger here?"

Carson nodded. "She's worked here for twelve years."

"Wow," Becca said. "That's cool."

"It sure is." I laughed. "I can't imagine my mom ever working in the park. Her idea of wilderness is when the gardener forgets to trim the hedges in our garden."

"Well then she definitely wouldn't like it at my house," Kayla said. "It used to be a barn."

Becca stared at her. "You *live* in a barn?"

Kayla laughed. "It's not really a barn anymore. It's been converted, so it's got windows and heat and all that stuff that most houses have. But it's still got lots of space and really high ceilings like a barn. My room's up on a balcony, where the hayloft used to be."

"That must be really nice," Carson commented. "I'd love to have lots of space. There are a lot of people in my family, so our house always seems crowded."

"My mother's an artist, so she needs lots of space and light to work," Kayla explained. "She has a studio in our house. Sometimes she paints outside, in our field."

I knew that Kayla's mom was an artist, but I had never been to her house. Even though we were in the same class, we weren't exactly close friends. I had a feeling that was going to change, though. *Just like Ranger Abe said, this trip is probably going to bring the five of us a lot closer together,* I realized.

"Hey, guess what? My mom got a call on her radio just as she was dropping me off," Carson said. "Someone reported hearing gunshots over in Rattlesnake Canyon."

"Do they think it might be the poachers?" Kayla asked, her voice filled with concern.

"Maybe," Carson replied. "My mom went over to meet Ranger Abe there to check it out." She paused. "Listen, you guys, before we go on this camping trip together, there's something I want to tell you, okay?"

"Sure, Carson, go ahead," I said, curious.

"Actually, Sophie already knows about this," Carson began. "But I want all of you to know. You see, I have a disability. A hearing disability."

"You mean you're deaf?" Becca blurted out. "But when you talk you sound so normal." Her cheeks colored. "Ooops, I didn't mean it that way, Carson. It's just that I thought deaf people were supposed to sound . . ."

"It's okay, Becca," Carson said calmly. "It's true that many deaf people do have trouble speaking clearly, partly because they can't hear themselves talk. For one thing, I'm not completely deaf. I do have some hearing in one ear. And I wear a hearing aid. But I've also had lots of years of speech therapy. I worked really hard to be able to speak this well."

I nodded. I was impressed. Carson had obviously had a lot to overcome in her life.

"Mostly I wanted all of you to know that in order to understand you I need to be able to see you when you talk," Carson explained.

"You mean so you can read our lips?" I asked her, putting it all together.

She nodded.

"Wow, Carson," Kayla said. "I'm really sorry to hear about that. I feel so bad for you."

"Don't," Carson responded. "The way I look at it, this is part of who I am. Besides, it has its advantages, too."

"Like what do you mean?" I asked her.

"Well, for one thing, I'm really clued into other stuff," Carson explained. "Visual stuff. I've got a really good memory for the way things look. For instance, I never forget a face."

"That's pretty cool," Becca said.

"There are definitely problems I have to overcome,

too, though," Carson went on. "Sometimes I have trouble locating things by sound. And that can be dangerous. Like when I can't tell which way traffic is coming from. So I have to be extra alert."

At the mention of traffic, I was reminded of the accident I'd had earlier. I looked down at my scraped knee. It had gotten a little bloodier.

Carson followed my gaze. "What happened to you, Alex?"

"Some crazy driver almost ran into me," I reported. "This car came barreling out of nowhere and ran me and my bike off the road into a ditch."

"That's terrible!" Kayla said.

"Are you okay?" Carson asked.

"Just that little scrape," I replied. "Other than that I'm fine. When Ranger Abe gets here I'll ask him for a bandage."

"I have a first aid kid in my pack," Carson offered. She opened her pack and pulled out a small white plastic box.

"Thanks," I said, taking it from her. I took out some cotton and antiseptic and started to clean my wound.

Just then I heard a voice from above me. "Aw, gee. Look at that."

I glanced up and saw two of the guys from the boys' division standing nearby. One of them I recognized as Rick, the boy who'd been so loud and obnoxious at the meeting last weekend. The other one was Sophie's brother, Jason.

"Just ignore them," Kayla said under her breath.

"Isn't that a shame, Jason," Rick continued in a

sarcastic tone. "The girls haven't even started the survival trip yet and already they have their first injury. Gee, I wonder if they're tough enough to make it out there."

"It's just a scraped knee," I retorted angrily. "It's no big deal." I was getting pretty sick of these two and their stupid remarks.

"Besides," Becca cracked. "From what I can see you two have a much more serious condition to worry about."

"Oh, yeah?" Jason asked. "What's that?"

"Shrunken brains," Becca replied.

I let out a little laugh. *Becca is really quick,* I thought. *These guys are no match for her.*

Just then Sophie came running into the parking lot. She had a worried expression on her face, and she looked pale.

"Hey, look, my sister decided to show up after all," Jason remarked. "I thought you chickened out, Sopp—I mean, Sophie."

"You guys," Sophie said breathlessly, "there's something really weird going on in the park back there. On my way here, as I was walking through the woods, I heard this really strange sound."

"What kind of sound?" I asked.

"I don't know," Sophie said, her voice shaking a little. "It sounded like . . . screeching."

"Screeching?" Kayla repeated.

Sophie nodded. "Yeah, it was really creepy. It was coming from somewhere in the woods."

"Screeching, huh?" Jason said. "What's the matter, Sophie, hearing ghosts already? Some people say Mesa del Oro is haunted by the ghost of an old prospector, you know. They say he died up there and his spirit haunts the park. Sure you still want to go?"

At his words, Sophie looked more nervous than ever.

"Don't listen to him, Sophie," I said. "It's just a stupid old story. It was probably just a bird you heard."

"But *maybe* it wasn't . . . ," Jason said, letting his voice trail off in a spooky way. "*Maybe* it was something else. . . ."

He and Rick started laughing.

"He's just trying to scare you, Sophie," Kayla said. "And I know why, too." She shot Jason a look. "It's an old fighting trick. Trying to reduce your own fear by making someone else feel more afraid than you do."

"*Me?* Afraid? That's crazy!" Jason responded. "I'm not afraid of anything!"

"Sure you are," Kayla replied. "You're afraid your sister is going to make a better ranger than you!"

"Oh, yeah, sure," Jason said. "Fat chance."

"Jason's right," Rick agreed. "There's no way any one of you will ever make as good a ranger as us."

"Well, I guess we'll just have to see about that," Kayla replied coolly.

Just then a green park jeep drove into the parking lot, and Ranger Abe got out. "Sorry I'm late, gang," he said. "I was over at Rattlesnake Canyon. Someone heard something over there, and we thought we might have our hunters. But it was a false alarm. We weren't able to find any sign of them in the canyon. Now, let's see if we can get you kids started on your trip. Let's go inside and get you your equipment."

We all filed through the door and followed him into the main meeting room. Inside were two stacks of tents, water canteens, and food packages.

"I guess these are ours," I said to Kayla, heading toward the smaller pile of equipment.

"These all are two-person tents," Ranger Abe told us. "There are three over there for the girls, and six here for the boys. In addition, you've got some food and some water. It's up to you how you want to ration your supplies. Remember, though, any food that you're storing overnight needs to be hung up in a tree so you don't have a problem with bears."

I glanced at Sophie. She licked her lips nervously.

"Okay, what else? Girls on the east side of the mountain, boys on the west," Ranger Abe went on. "Oh, and let me make sure you all know where the alarm button is. Follow me."

He led us back outside and took us around to the side of the building. A small glass box was mounted there. Inside was a white plastic panel with a red button marked EMERGENCY ONLY.

"If there's an emergency after the park closes at seven o'clock, or if any of you decides you can't make it through and you want to leave before the night is over, this is the button to press," Ranger Abe explained.

"Oh, good." Sophie sighed behind me. "That makes me feel better."

I had to admit, it made me feel better, too. It was strange to think we would be on our own in the park after hours. At least we knew there was some way we could get help if there were a real emergency.

"Of course, I have to warn you that pressing the button in a nonemergency and quitting the camping trip means giving up your place in the junior rangers as well," Ranger Abe added solemnly. "After all, the idea of the survival trip is to be resourceful, to solve whatever problems come up on your own if possible." He laughed a little. "So try to avoid using the 'panic button' unless you absolutely have to."

Jason laughed. "Hey, 'the panic button,' did you hear that, Sophie? Why don't you just press it now and get it over with?"

A bunch of the guys laughed.

"All right, all right, that's enough," Ranger Abe said. "You kids better get going before the sun starts to get low. Go on inside and pack up your gear, and then you can head out to the mountain. If you check your maps you'll see that the trail splits going up. The girls will take the east trail, and the boys will take the west trail." He smiled. "And I'll see you all back here tomorrow morning. Good luck!"

THIRTEEN

Carson's blue vinyl backpack swayed and bobbed just ahead of me as I followed her up the east trail of Mesa del Oro. Directly behind me, Sophie was singing a song I recognized from the radio.

I twisted to look at her. "Hey, what is that?"

She stopped singing, and her face went white. "What? Did you hear something?"

"No, no," I laughed. "I meant what was that song you were just singing?"

Sophie laughed, too. "Oh, I guess I'm a little jumpy."

"Great title," Becca cracked from her place in line behind Sophie. "Is there a dance that goes with that, too?"

Sophie laughed again. "Actually, it was 'As Bad as It Gets,' by Problem Child."

"Sounds more like a description of your brother Jason than a song to me," Becca commented.

"That's for sure!" Sophie said. "I think they must have had him in mind when they wrote it."

We continued climbing, and I shivered a little in my T-shirt. Already the air was cool, and I knew it would only be a matter of time before the sun went behind the mountain, leaving us in total shade. *We'd probably better find someplace to set up camp pretty soon,* I realized.

A few minutes later, we came to a slight clearing in the trees. I put my hand on Carson's arm. She stopped and turned around. Sophie, Becca, and Kayla joined us in the clearing.

"What do you guys think?" I asked. "Should we stop here? The ground looks nice and level. And there's definitely enough room for our three tents and a camp-fire."

"Looks great to me," Kayla agreed.

"Let's go for it," Carson declared.

Becca let her backpack drop. "I'm starved. I say let's open the food."

"We'd probably better build the fire and set up the tents first," I told her. "Before it gets too dark to see what we're doing."

"I've never made a fire before," Becca said.

"That's okay, I'll do it," I replied. "You start on one of the tents."

She laughed. "Actually, I've never set up a tent before, either. We don't exactly do a lot of camping in New York. But I guess it's better to make a mistake with the tent than the fire. At least if I set up a tent wrong it can't kill us!"

"I'll help you with the fire, Alex," Kayla volunteered.

"Great, let's gather some kindling," I told her.

Kayla and I scoured the campground area for sticks

and twigs. Meanwhile Sophie, Carson, and Becca started unpacking the three tents.

After just a few moments, there was a cry of exasperation from Sophie. "I just can't figure this thing out!"

I turned to look at her. She was standing in a tangle of nylon, string, and tent poles.

"What's wrong?" I asked.

"My tent doesn't make any sense!" she replied.

I walked over to her. "Let me take a look at it."

The tent was a pretty simple design. I could see that it was supposed to be supported by three collapsible poles, two long ones across the middle and one short one near the entrance.

I inserted the two long poles through their seams, crisscrossing them in the center, and fastened them at the ends near the bottom of the tent.

"Now, the third pole should go right here," I told Sophie, pointing to the area near the entrance to the tent that was still unsupported.

"What third pole?" she said.

"The third one," I said again. "The short one. The only one left."

"Alex, there is no third pole," Sophie said.

"Are you sure?" I asked her. *That didn't make sense.*

Carson, who had finished setting up her tent, noticed what was happening and walked over to us.

"What's going on?" she asked.

"There might be a pole missing," I told her. "Check the tent bag," I said to Sophie.

Sophie picked up the bag and shook it. "Nothing."

"What? But that can't be!" I checked the bag myself. It was empty. "I can't believe it," I said. "There's a pole missing. No wonder you were having so much trouble setting this up."

"Hey, maybe there's a pole missing from my tent, too," Becca called. "Because I'm sure not getting anywhere with this." She laughed. "Or maybe it's just because I'm a city girl."

"Hang on, I'll help you," I said. I walked over to her. Becca had already managed to feed the two longer poles through their seams and fit the ends in place.

"This is pretty good," I told Becca. "All you have to do is put the third one in." I put my hand in the tent bag. To my astonishment, it was empty! "This is totally weird!" I said. "Yours is missing, too, Becca."

Kayla walked over from the campfire. "Hey, I know! Maybe this is part of the survival test! You know, to kind of make it tougher."

"No way," Carson put in, "I don't think Ranger Abe would do that."

"I agree," I said. "After all, he said we'd have *minimal* equipment up here, not *defective* equipment."

"Besides," Carson pointed out, "*my* tent is complete."

"Ranger Abe did have his hands full with the poachers and everything," Becca pointed out. "Maybe he just didn't get a chance to check the equipment."

"Yeah, I guess it was just an accident," Sophie said.

"I wouldn't say that, either," I replied. I did some quick calculating. "With all the parts to these tents, I'd say the mathematical probability of both tents *accidentally* missing the exact same piece is about one in thirty."

"You mean there's a one-in-thirty chance that this could happen by mistake?" Carson asked.

I nodded.

"So then what are you trying to say, Alex?" Kayla asked. "That someone removed the two poles from the tents? Why?"

"*That* I *don't* have the answer for," I replied.

"Do you really think someone took them?" Carson asked.

"They *are* pretty small poles," Kayla pointed out. "And they do collapse. Someone could have done it pretty easily without being noticed."

"I'm not saying that's what happened for sure," I cautioned. "But it does seem like an awfully big coincidence."

"Well, coincidence or not, we have a bigger problem now," Sophie said. She pointed to the two half-collapsed tents. "We can't possibly sleep in these things tonight. And we can't all fit in Carson's tent, either."

"Sophie's right," Becca agreed. "Where are we all going to sleep?"

"Don't worry," I said. "I'm sure I can rig something up."

I walked over to my pack and took out a couple of bungee cords. I looped the ends together to make one big cord and tossed it over a low-hanging branch. I fastened one end to the droopy part of Sophie's tent.

"Now, Becca, if you just pull your tent over here, we can attach this end to it," I explained. "That way the two tents can support each other in the front."

Becca and Kayla pulled the tent closer. I looped the end of the bungee onto it. It wasn't perfect—the tents were still sagging a bit in a couple of spots—but it would definitely work for the night.

"Cool," Becca said admiringly.

I grinned. "Never go anywhere without bungees, that's what I always say. You never know when you might need one."

"Is it time to eat now?" Sophie asked. "I'm really starved."

"Yeah, let's put something on that fire before it goes out," I agreed.

Carson opened one of the food containers and peered inside. "Well, there are some noodles in here. We could cook them in a little of our water."

"Plain noodles?" Sophie complained. "Doesn't sound too appetizing."

Carson went back to the food. "There's a can of tuna in here, too," she reported. "And some powdered milk. We could mix it all together and make tuna casserole."

"Um, do you think we could keep mine plain?" Kayla asked. "I'm a vegetarian, and I don't eat fish."

"I have an even better idea," Becca said, a mischievous look on her face. "How about putting some homemade Alfredo sauce on those noodles?"

I laughed. "Sounds great, but where are we supposed to get that?"

"How about right here?" Becca dug into her pack and took out a parcel wrapped in newspaper. She removed the newspaper. Inside was a plastic container filled with creamy liquid.

"You brought Alfredo sauce in your backpack? You must be kidding!" Kayla said.

Becca shook her head. "No, actually, this is one of those rare moments when I'm *not*." She laughed. "And it's not even the third Tuesday of the month!"

"Where did you get that stuff?" I asked her.

"My stepfather made it," she replied. "He and my mom have a new restaurant, the Cayenga Grill. This was left over from last night's special. He gave it to me when I was leaving the restaurant this afternoon." She chuckled. "You see, my stepdad has a motto a little bit like yours, Alex. 'Never go anywhere without a gourmet sauce. You never know when you might need one.'"

We all laughed.

"Still, I can't believe you carried that extra weight all the way up the mountain in your pack," I said.

Becca held up the container and grinned at me. "When you taste this, you'll understand why," she promised.

After dinner, we all sat around the fire, watching the embers die out. The moon was nearly full, and the moonlight shone into the clearing, illuminating everything with a silver glow.

"That was the most incredible pasta sauce I've ever had," Sophie said.

"Delicious," I agreed. I closed my eyes. I felt tired and full.

"Mmmm, I'd love to have some marshmallows to toast right about now," Carson said dreamily.

"Hey, don't look at me for that one," Becca replied. "S'mores aren't on the menu at the Cayenga Grill."

We all laughed.

I opened my eyes. "I guess we'd better wrap up the rest of the food and put it up in a tree."

"Oh, right," Kayla agreed. "Remember what Ranger Abe said about bears."

"Please!" Sophie cried. "Don't remind me!"

"We can put it in my daypack," Carson offered. "Then we can hang it from a branch."

We all packed up the food and put it into Carson's pack. Carson gave Becca a boost, and she hung the pack from a branch about seven feet off the ground.

Sophie stood under the tree, looking up at the branch. "What I want to know is, if it's so safe up there in the tree, why are we all sleeping down here in these tents tonight?"

We all laughed.

I yawned. "Speaking of sleep, I think I'll get into my sleeping bag. I'm beat."

Kayla toed the embers of the fire with her hiking boot. "The fire's out anyway. We all might as well go to bed before we get too cold."

Suddenly, I thought I heard something coming from the woods.

"*Oooooaaaa . . .*"

I paused. Had I really heard something? *Maybe it was just the wind,* I thought.

But then I heard it again. "*Ooooooaaaaa . . .*" It sounded like a low moan.

"What was that?" Kayla asked, alert.

"I don't know," I whispered. "I heard it, too."

"Oh, no," Sophie wailed softly.

"*Oooooooaaaaaaaaaaaa . . .*"

"There it is again," Kayla said.

"I heard it that time, too," Becca added.

We were all silent a moment, waiting. Sophie gripped my arm.

"What's going on?" Carson asked. "What kind of sound is it?"

"It's kind of like a moan," I reported. "Like . . ." *Like what?* I tried to think. "Like some kind of animal growling, maybe."

"Like maybe a bear growling," Sophie added in a shaky voice.

Everyone was silent.

"I don't hear it anymore," Becca whispered.

"Maybe it wasn't anything," Kayla said hopefully.

"Maybe it went away," I added. Still, my heart was pounding. I gazed around at the dark trees.

Suddenly there was another sound—a high-pitched wail.

"*Eeeeeeeiiiiiiiiiiiiiiii!*"

Sophie let out a scream.

I grabbed Carson's hand.

We all froze.

FOURTEEN

"What was that awful noise?" Kayla asked in a hushed tone.

"That was no bear!" Sophie said, her voice shaking with fear. "Oh my gosh, what if it's that dead prospector?"

"Sophie, it can't be the dead prospector," I reminded her. "The dead prospector is *dead*."

"You know what I mean," she replied. "His ghost! Maybe it's his ghost!"

"There is no such thing as ghosts," I told her in as calm a voice as I could. "I'm sure there's a perfectly logical explanation for this. There has to be." *Only problem is, I can't think of what it might be,* I added silently. I swallowed nervously. I don't like it when I can't figure things out. Then I thought of something. "Sophie, did that sound like what you said you heard in the woods earlier today?"

Sophie shook her head.

"Are you sure?" Carson asked.

Sophie nodded. "This sound is definitely different. Although I can't say I'm too crazy about either one of them."

I tried to think. I knew there had to be a logical explanation. Even so, I couldn't help feeling sort of nervous myself. *After all,* I reasoned, *just because there's a logical explanation doesn't mean I'm going to like it when I find out what it is.*

"Eeeeeeeiiiiiiiiiiiiiiii!"

We all crouched together, waiting.

"I heard that one," Carson said. "They must be getting louder."

I nodded.

"Which means whatever it is must be getting closer," Kayla pointed out.

Becca put her head in her hands. "Nothing like this ever happened to me back in New York!" she said miserably.

"What should we do?" Sophie asked, her expression panicky. "Run?"

"Maybe we should wait it out," I suggested, my heart pounding in my chest. "Maybe it will go away." But the truth was I didn't have much hope. I didn't have any idea what this thing was, or how it might feel about us. Mentally, I went over everything I'd ever read about wild animals. *I know that if a bear approaches you you're supposed to pretend you're dead. Does that work for other animals, too?*

"Eeeeeeeiiiiiiiiiiiiiiii!"

Suddenly, the expression on Sophie's face changed from fear to recognition.

"I *do* know that last sound!" she announced, straightening up. "And *not* from the woods earlier today, either. *Jason!*"

I heard laughter from the woods, followed by rapid footsteps.

"I can't believe it!" I cried. "It's the boys!"

"Those rats!" Carson cried. "They're running away. I can feel the vibrations of their feet on the ground!"

"Let's get them!" Becca yelled.

We all took off into the woods in the direction that the sounds had come from. After a minute or two of searching, I saw a flash of white between two trees.

"This way!" I called. "I see them!" I tugged on Carson's arm.

The figure disappeared, and I heard laughter in the distance.

"They're getting away!" Kayla yelled.

"Let's hurry!" Becca urged.

But the woods were silent now.

"Jason!" Sophie yelled. "Come out, you big chicken!"

There was no movement in the trees.

"Forget it," I said, panting. "They're gone."

"Come on," Kayla said. "Let's go back to camp."

I looked around, a little disoriented by the chase through the woods. "Which way is it?"

"I remember the way. Follow me," Carson said, leading us through the woods.

A few minutes later I spotted the tents in the distance, between the trees.

"I can't believe the boys were trying to scare us off the mountain," Becca said incredulously.

"I can," Sophie replied. "I bet Jason and Rick would do anything to make us look bad."

"Well, no one's going to scare *me* away, that's for sure," Kayla announced.

"Me either," I said with determination.

A few yards from our campsite, Carson stopped in her tracks.

I walked up alongside her and touched her arm. "What is it, Carson?"

She pointed up to the trees. "The food bag! It's gone!"

"It can't be!" I said.

"Well, it isn't up in the tree anymore," Carson replied.

"Maybe it fell," Kayla suggested.

We all hurried to the campsite and began to search the ground around the tree. But it was no use. The daypack filled with food had disappeared.

"What if a bear got to it after all?" Sophie asked.

"I don't think so," I told her. "A bear would probably have tried to rip open the pack to get at the food right away. Whoever took it just grabbed the whole thing and ran."

"Maybe the boys did it," Becca suggested.

"But how could they?" Kayla asked. "We were just chasing them through the woods!"

"We don't know how many of them were in the woods just now," I pointed out. "It would only have taken one of them to hide out here and wait until we left to take the pack."

"That's true," Becca said thoughtfully.

Just then I heard a familiar rumbling sound from the direction of the road just below the mountain.

"That's a car engine starting!" I said quickly. "Someone's down there!"

"But the park is closed!" Carson said. "Who would be driving around the mountain roads after dark?"

"Let's go find out!" Kayla cried.

We raced down the trail in the dark, toward the road. After a few moments I spotted two taillights glowing red in the distance, disappearing around the bend in the road.

"We missed it," I said, slowing down. "It's gone."

We all stopped and stared off in the direction where the car's lights had disappeared.

"Do you think whoever that was is the same person who took our food?" Becca asked.

I shrugged. "No way of telling for sure." Then I had a thought. "I guess it could have been poachers, though."

"Sure," Kayla agreed. "Maybe they sneaked into the park at night and came up here on the mountain to set traps. They probably didn't even realize we were here until they saw our campsite."

"But why did they take our food?" Sophie asked.

"Maybe they were looking for leftover Alfredo sauce," Becca said, forcing a little laugh.

"Whatever the reason, it means we don't have any food left," Carson pointed out.

"That's right," Kayla said. "What should we do? We can't say up here without food."

"We'll be fine for the rest of the night," I said. "It's true that we have no food left, but at least no one's hungry for now."

"What if the poachers are nearby?" Sophie asked. "What if they come back?"

"If they were poachers, they've probably already set their traps or done whatever they came up on the mountain to do. Chances are they won't come back to this area again tonight," I pointed out. "As long as we watch out for traps and are careful about where we walk, we should be fine."

"I agree with Alex," Kayla said. "We can report everything we heard and saw first thing in the morning. Let's not give up yet."

"No way, I'm not giving up *ever*," Sophie agreed.

I stared at her in surprise. "I thought you were the one who was so scared."

"I was," Sophie said. "And I still am. But that doesn't mean I want to give up, either. I say let's finish the trip and spend the rest of the night on the mountain."

Slowly, we turned and headed back up the trail toward our campsite. As we walked, I turned things over in my head. *There have definitely been a lot of weird things going on since we got here,* I decided. *Actually, starting when I first became a junior ranger just a week ago. First there was that strange phone message for me, and now all this.* I wondered what it meant.

As we followed the path back toward our campsite, Carson suddenly stopped and let out a gasp.

"What is it?" I asked, turning to look at her.

Carson didn't answer. Her gaze was fixed at something

directly behind me. Her face was pale in the moonlight, and it wore a horrified expression. She pointed, still speechless.

I turned to see what it was, and my heart leapt into my throat.

There, pinned to the trunk of a tree with a knife, was a green Cayenga Park cap!

KAYLA

FIFTEEN

I stared straight ahead, barely able to believe my eyes. Someone had stabbed a knife through a Cayenga Park baseball cap and stuck it to a tree! The sight of it made my blood boil.

"What kind of creep would do something like that?" I asked with disgust.

"Obviously someone who's trying to scare us," Alex remarked in a low voice.

And from the looks of things, it's working, I thought, looking around at Becca's, Sophie's, Carson's, and Alex's faces.

"Well, *I*, for one, refuse to be scared," I announced. "In fact, I think we should get to the bottom of this right away." I was sick of weird noises, sick of cars driving around the park when they weren't supposed to, sick of stupid pranks and everything else. "I say we go straight to the campsite and get the flashlights so we can thoroughly investigate this area."

"Investigate for what, Kayla?" Becca asked nervously.

"For clues," I replied. "We have to figure out who did this awful thing, and who took our food, too."

"Do you think this could all be the work of the boys?" Carson asked.

"I don't know," Alex replied. She indicated the cap and the knife. "This is pretty harsh, even for them. Besides, we did hear that car."

"Some of the kids in the boys' division are old enough to drive," Carson reminded us.

"I don't think it was them," Sophie said. "My brother can be pretty nasty, but I don't think even he and Rick would do something like this."

"Who else would want to scare us, though?" Becca asked.

"That's what I'd like to know," I said.

"I agree with Kayla," Alex said. "Let's go get the flashlights and see what else we can find."

We headed back to the campsite.

"I've got a flashlight in my pack," Carson volunteered.

"Me too." I walked over to the tent that Alex had helped Becca set up earlier. "My pack's right in here."

I unzipped the tent and opened the flap. But when I looked inside, I saw something that made me jump back in surprise. There, staring back at me, were two glowing green eyes.

I gasped and stumbled backward.

"What is it, Kayla?" Sophie asked me.

"I think it's an animal of some kind," I replied.

"An animal?" Becca echoed.

"But how did it get in there? Your tent was *zipped*," Alex pointed out.

With the others behind me, I moved toward the tent again, ever so slowly. Suddenly, the animal raced past me.

"It's a raccoon!" Carson cried.

The raccoon, realizing it was surrounded, began to panic. It darted back and forth in a frenzy. Finally it backed up near a hollow log. It opened its mouth, hissing at us with a fierce expression on its face.

"Oh my gosh! What's wrong with it?" Becca asked.

"I think it's sick," I said. Looking at the raccoon made me feel really sorry for it. Its eyes were fiery, and a thick white foam dripped from its mouth. There was definitely something very wrong with it.

"Rabies," Carson said in a low voice. "It's got rabies. Everyone be careful."

I regarded the animal carefully. I knew that sometimes sick animals were more likely to attack than healthy ones, especially if they felt trapped. I tried to think of what to do. I heard my father's voice in my head. *Stay alert.* That's what he always said when we were sparring during karate class at the dojo. *Wait for your chance.* I just had to think of this raccoon as my opponent. I had to do the same thing I would in class—be smarter and faster than the opponent and use his own weaknesses against him.

I watched carefully as the raccoon backed up, still hissing at us and frothing.

"Chase it!" Sophie suggested. "Maybe it will run away."

"No," I cautioned in a low voice. "It might get even more scared and attack."

The raccoon continued to back up, moving into the log for safety. *This is it!* I realized. *My chance!* The back end of the log was already blocked by a large rock. My eyes darted left and then right for something to block the front end. I spotted Alex's frame backpack nearby. *Go!*

With a quick roundhouse kick, my right leg arching through the air, I sent the backpack flying. It landed right on target, blocking the entrance to the hole.

"Wow!" Becca exclaimed. "That was the coolest!"

"Quick!" Alex cried. "Get some rocks to fortify it!"

We scrambled for rocks and piled them up against the backpack, trapping the raccoon.

Can it breathe in there? I wondered, feeling a pang of guilt. I didn't want the animal to suffer more than it already had.

As if in answer, a pair of small dark hands and a pointed nose appeared in the crack between the top of the log and the pack. Seeing them, my heart felt like it was about to break.

"Rabies!" I said in disbelief, remembering the strange message that had been left on the phone machine on my house. "I can't believe it. So that message was right!"

Alex stared at me. "You got a call about rabies in the park, too?"

"Me too!" Becca exclaimed. "Some ranger called my house!"

"The same thing happened to me!" Sophie cried. "I didn't think it was real, though. I thought it was just my brother, pulling another one of his tricks."

"What are you all talking about?" Carson asked.

"Apparently there's been some kind of rabies problem in the park," I explained. "One of the rangers called my house to tell me about it last week, but I wasn't home. I didn't think it was serious, though, because when my dad called the park to find out about it they said there wasn't a problem after all."

"The same thing happened to me!" Becca said.

"You guys," Carson said, "there is no rabies problem in the park. If there were, I would have heard about it. My mom's a ranger, remember?"

"Carson's right," Alex said. "I checked the records on the computer. There hasn't been a case of rabies here for years!"

Becca pointed to the raccoon nose poking out from behind the backpack. "Well, then, what do you call *that*?"

We all stared at the log and the backpack. No one knew what to say.

"Poor thing," I said softly. I turned to the others. "I don't think it's right to leave it suffering like this all night. Someone has to help it, or else put it out of its misery."

"Maybe we should go press the panic button after all," Becca suggested.

"And give up being in the junior rangers? No way!" Sophie objected.

"Ranger Abe will probably understand," Becca said. "If we explain that we did it for the raccoon."

"Wait a minute, you guys," I said. "Let's stop and think. Remember, Ranger Abe said he wants us to try to solve problems without using the panic button if we can. That's the whole point of the survival trip."

"I don't know," Carson said. "This seems like a pretty big problem to try to solve on our own."

I thought a moment. "I have an idea. What about that guy who lives in the park? The one Ranger Abe introduced us to at the first meeting?"

"Oh yeah," Sophie said with enthusiasm. "Didn't Ranger Abe say that guy worked with wildlife? Maybe he can help the raccoon."

"Good idea," Becca agreed. "But where can we find him?"

"Dr. Burr! Ranger Abe said he lived at a special study center in the woods, beyond the public campground," Alex remembered.

"There are a few old buildings up in that area," Carson volunteered. "It's probably one of them."

"Maybe it's on the map of the park," Alex suggested. "I'll get mine and check." She paused. "Oh, wait a minute. It's in there." She pointed to her pack, which was still blocking the hollow log. I could hear the raccoon scratching at the pack from the other side. *Poor thing,* I thought again. *We've got to help it.*

"I'll get my map," I volunteered. I crawled into my tent and dug in my pack. I took out the map, my flashlight, and a sweatshirt.

I came back out and pulled on my sweatshirt, and we all gathered around the map.

"There! I bet that's it!" Carson said.

I squinted at the map and shone my flashlight onto the area where she was pointing. There, between the campground and the vineyard, was a small gray rectangle meant to represent a building.

I looked up at the eager circle of faces around me. I could still hear the scratching of the raccoon in the background.

"Come on, you guys," I said. "Let's go!"

SIXTEEN

I led the way with the map and the flashlight as we crept down the mountain trail. *I wish we could go faster,* I thought, as the image of the suffering raccoon filled my head. *But it's too dangerous. If those were poachers who were up here on the mountain earlier, there could be traps all around us. We can't take the chance of stepping on one of them.*

The moon shone above us and filtered down through the leaves of the trees, leaving speckled shadows on the ground around us. Somewhere in the distance an owl hooted.

"What was that?" Becca asked behind me.

"Nothing," I answered. "Just an owl." I thought about a Native American legend my grandmother used to tell me about. My mom's mom is part Native American, part Mexican-American, and she knows a bunch of really great old stories. In this story, a woman was turned into an owl as a punishment for being selfish. I remember that it used to confuse me when I was a little girl. The way I saw it, being turned into an owl wouldn't be a punishment at all. I guess that's because when I was little my biggest wish was to be able to fly.

I wouldn't mind being able to fly right now, either, I thought as we followed the trail around past the public campground area and up a steep hill toward the vineyard.

I stopped for a moment to check the map again. Becca, Kayla, Sophie, and Carson clustered around me.

"It should be just up here, through these woods," I said, shining my flashlight ahead on the trail.

Just then a terrible sound pierced the night air.

"Eeeeeeeee! Eeeeeeeeeeeee!"

What was that? I wondered, my heart beating faster. It sounded like a very high-pitched shriek.

We all froze.

"That was it! That was it!" Sophie said breathlessly.

"What?" Alex asked her.

"That was the sound!" Sophie replied. "The screeching sound I heard earlier today on my way to park headquarters!"

"Are you sure you heard the same thing both times?" Carson asked.

"Positive," Sophie replied. She shivered a little. "I'd know that sound anywhere. It gives me the creeps."

"I think it came from up there," I said, nodding in the direction of the woods ahead of us.

As if in answer, we heard the sound again.

"Eeeeeeeee! Eeeeeeeeeeeee!"

"Is that a person, or an animal?" Becca asked nervously.

I swallowed. "Only one way to find out."

We continued up through the woods, walking close together. As we walked, I kept an eye out for traps—and for any other surprises that might be lurking among the dark trees.

I stepped on a branch, and it snapped under my foot with a crack.

Becca jumped and gasped at the sound, and then covered her mouth. "Oh my gosh, that scared me!"

"Look," Carson whispered suddenly. "Up there. It's a building."

Ahead of us, partly concealed by the dense forest, was a small building. There were no lights on anywhere.

The screeching started again, louder this time.

"Eeeeeeeee! Eeeeeeeeeeeeee!"

"I think it's coming from inside," Alex breathed.

"Come on, let's go see," I whispered back.

My mind was racing as we crept closer to the building. It looked as if no one was there. *Unless Dr. Burr is sleeping,* I thought. *But how could anyone possibly sleep with that awful sound? Or maybe Dr. Burr is in some kind of trouble,* I realized. *What if the same people who took our food and put the knife through that cap on the tree have done something to him?*

When we reached the building, it was clear that the high-pitched sound was coming from somewhere inside.

"What should we do?" Becca asked.

"Let's try the door," Alex suggested.

We crept around the dark building until we got to a wooden door. A sign was nailed to the outside of it.

WILDLIFE RESEARCH CENTER
DR. LYLE BURR
WARNING: SENSITIVE EXPERIMENTAL
MATERIALS WITHIN
KEEP OUT!

"It says 'keep out,'" Carson said doubtfully.

"Forget it," I replied. "Someone or something in there is definitely hurt." I knew I would never forgive myself if I didn't try to do the right thing. "We have to go in." I reached out and tried the doorknob. "It's locked!"

"What about the windows?" Alex suggested.

"Good idea," Sophie replied.

We crept around the building, trying the dark, dust-covered windows. But every single one of them was locked.

I breathed on a pane of glass and rubbed the dirt away with a corner of my sweatshirt. I put my face close to the window. To my surprise, I couldn't see a thing.

"It looks like the window is covered with cardboard on the inside," I told the others.

Becca ran to check another window. "This one is, too!"

"They all are!" Alex called from a third window.

I had a really bad feeling about all this. "Someone or something is in terrible trouble inside that building, and it's up to us to help," I said.

"But how?" Sophie asked. "We can't get in!"

Just then the screeching started again.

"Eeeeeeee! Eeeeeeeeeeee! Eeeeeeeeeeeeeeeeeeee!"

I knew I had to do something. I couldn't just stand by

and listen to this awful sound. I pulled off my sweatshirt and wrapped it around my right hand to protect it.

"Stand back!" I yelled to the others. "I'm going to break the glass!"

"Be careful!" Sophie cautioned.

I pulled my right elbow back, placing my punching arm into chamber, as it's called in karate. I took a deep breath and concentrated on focusing all of my power into my hand. In one movement, I propelled my arm forward and turned my face away from the glass, letting out a loud *kiai* as I punched.

"Eeeeeow!"

The glass splintered with a cracking sound. Several pieces fell to the ground.

"Cool!" Becca breathed.

"Come on," I said, clearing the leftover shards of broken glass from the window frame with my sweatshirt.

Together, the five of us tore frantically at the cardboard on the other side of the window. When we had cleared it away, I picked up my flashlight and directed its beam inside.

What I saw shocked and sickened me.

The room beyond the window was filled with cages of raccoons. The cages were tiny, and the animals were stacked on top of one another. Most of them looked sick, and they were obviously suffering.

"Oh my gosh," I gasped. I felt tears come to my eyes.

As I moved the beam of my light across the cages, I could see that several of the raccoons inside had a stump in place of one of their paws, as if they had been caught in traps. Many of the animals were foaming at the mouth, like the one we had found back at our campsite.

Rabies, I said to myself. *They all have rabies.*

Beside me, Sophie let out a cry and turned away.

"I can't believe it," Carson murmured. "What kind of experiment is this supposed to be?"

I couldn't take my eyes off the animals. Row after row of green eyes stared back at me from the cramped cages. I spotted one raccoon pacing frantically in its tiny cage, biting at the metal bars. A moment later, it began screeching with panic.

"Eeeeeeeee! Eeeeeeeeeeeee!"

Dr. Burr was nowhere in sight.

I pulled myself away from the window and faced the others.

"We have to report this immediately," I said. "Whatever Dr. Burr is doing with these animals, it's *not* research. Not *real* research, at least. I'm sure Ranger Abe has no idea about any of this."

"You're right, Kayla," Alex responded. "It looks like Dr. Burr's been the one trapping animals in the park."

"He may even be the person who's been trying to sabotage us," Sophie added. "I think we should—"

"Wait a minute," Carson interrupted. She sniffed the air. "I smell fire!" she cried. She spun quickly and sniffed again. "And it's coming from the direction of the mountain!"

We all hurried down the path through the woods to get a clearer view of the mountain. Sure enough, a thick cloud of smoke was visible in the moonlight. And it was coming straight from Mesa del Oro!

SEVENTEEN

"Wait a minute, what about the boys?" Alex gasped suddenly. "They're still up there!"

"They must have smelled it by now," Becca said. "They're probably already on their way down the mountain."

"Not necessarily," Alex replied. She put up one hand to check the breeze. "The wind is blowing to the southeast. Which means the smoke is blowing that way, too, toward *us*. The boys are on the west side of the mountain. They may not have smelled the smoke yet. They're probably still up there, asleep in their tents!"

"We have to warn them!" Sophie cried. "My brother may be a pain, but I don't want him to *die*!"

"I think we'd better split up," Alex decided. "I'll run to park headquarters and press the panic button to call the rangers. Someone else should warn the boys."

I turned to Becca and Carson. "The three of us can go

check out the fire. Maybe there's something we can do to contain it somehow."

Carson nodded.

"You got it," Becca agreed.

We all took off down the trail. When we reached the bottom, Alex and Sophie turned left to head for the trails that led to the east side of the mountain and park headquarters.

The smell of smoke grew stronger as Carson, Becca, and I raced toward the trail that led up the western side of the mountain.

Suddenly I thought of the raccoon, trapped inside the hollow log at our campsite. *If the fire reaches that raccoon, it will be all our fault!* I thought miserably. *But I suppose we had no choice but to trap it like that. Otherwise it could have bitten one of us.* Still, I felt terrible when I thought of that poor sick animal trapped in the log with the fire right nearby. I pushed myself to run harder.

We reached the part of the trail that ran alongside the road. The air was thick with smoke now, and the three of us started coughing. I pulled the neck of my T-shirt up to cover my nose and mouth and help filter out some of the smoke.

Suddenly, above the noise of our coughing, I heard a familiar sound. At first I thought it might be the roar of the fire, which didn't seem like it could be too far off now. But then I realized it wasn't the fire at all.

"There's a car coming!" I yelled through my T-shirt. I grabbed Carson's and Becca's arms and pointed toward the road. "A car!"

Before I could say another word, the car came into view. It was moving at top speed, weaving all over the road.

"Watch out!" Carson yelled as the car veered toward us.

The three of us jumped back off the trail into the woods. To my astonishment, the car lost control and kept coming until it crashed into the trees directly in front of us and came to a stop.

Carson, Becca, and I hurried back onto the trail and crossed through the trees to the car. Its front end was crushed like an accordion, and a thin column of black smoke rose from under the hood. The driver was slumped over the wheel, motionless.

"Come on!" Becca yelled. "Help me!" She pulled open the driver's side door, and we rushed to her side. Together we lifted the driver's head and shoulders from the steering wheel and leaned them back against the seat.

"It's Dr. Burr!" Carson gasped.

Dr. Burr's forehead was cut, and he was unconscious. The three of us managed to pull him out of the car and lay him on the grass.

"He needs CPR," Becca said. "I'll do it, I know how. You guys go on without me."

I nodded, coughing. The smoke was getting thicker now, and my eyes were stinging. Carson and I ran back to the trail. Together we rushed on up the mountainside.

Soon I could feel the heat of the fire on my face and hear the roar of the flames in my ears. The sky was glowing with light from the fire. I was choking on the smoke. I felt as if I could barely breathe.

After a few moments, I saw the red-orange glow of the fire in the distance. I gulped for air and tried to push myself to keep going. But soon it became clear that the heat was too strong.

I turned to Carson helplessly. She too was choking on the thick black smoke, and her face was smeared with ash from the air.

I tried to think of what to do. Suddenly I remembered the public campground, only a mile to the southeast of the mountain. If the wind really was headed in that direction, it would spread the fire that way, too. I also knew that any serious damage to the campground would be terrible for the park.

The roar of the flames was getting louder in my ears. We didn't have much longer before the fire would reach us.

Suddenly, I had an idea. *If we move ahead of the fire and try to dig a trench at the southeastern base of the mountain, maybe we can slow the fire down and save the campground. If we clear away as much of the brush there as possible the fire won't have as much to burn,* I decided.

I called out to Carson. "Let's head down to the base! Maybe we can clear away some brush and dig a trench!" But I could barely even hear my own voice. *It's no use,* I thought, *the sound of the fire is too loud.*

To my amazement, Carson nodded.

She heard me! I thought incredulously. *But how could she?* Then I remembered. *Carson doesn't rely on her hearing to begin with. The sound of the fire is no extra problem for her at all. She understood what I was saying because she was reading my lips!*

I nodded back to Carson. She motioned for me to head with her for the eastern base of the mountain. Together we ran through the woods.

The air was a little clearer at the base of the mountain, and I gulped at it, trying to clear my lungs. My eyes were still tearing, and the tears were spilling down my cheeks.

"Come on!" Carson yelled, grabbing a pile of dry leaves. "Let's clear as much as we can before the fire gets down this far!"

I was exhausted. Part of me just wanted to run away from this mountain, to go somewhere where the air would be clear and I could lie down and catch my breath. But I knew we couldn't give up now. *If this fire spreads it could wipe out the campground, or even the entire park,* I reminded myself. *Hundreds, probably thousands, of trees and animals are depending on us.*

I went down on my hands and knees and put every ounce of energy I could muster into clearing away the dry sticks, leaves, and branches in front of me. I knew if we could just clear away a big enough area, we had a chance of slowing down the fire.

Desperately I clawed at the earth beneath me, pulling up roots. Sweat was pouring down my face, and my arms and my shoulders were aching.

I could hear the fire getting closer. *It's no use,* I thought. *We'll never do it.* Still, I continued, grabbing at the leaves and roots. I choked on the smoke, exhausted.

Don't give up, I told myself. *No matter what, just keep going.*

Suddenly, I felt a large, gloved hand on my shoulder. I turned and gazed upward. A firefighter was standing right over me! I stared at him in disbelief. I realized I could hear the whir of helicopters above me.

"We'll take over from here," the firefighter said.

I looked around and saw dozens more firefighters headed up the mountain. Relieved, I sank into the ground, gasping for air.

A moment later, a woman in a white medic's uniform approached me and helped me to my feet.

"Can you walk?" she asked me.

I nodded, unable to speak. My throat and eyes were burning.

The medic helped me back down the trail to the road, where I saw two ambulances, their red lights flashing in the night. She helped me over to one of the ambulances. Its rear doors were open, and Carson was sitting in the back with a clear plastic oxygen mask over her nose and mouth. Out of the corner of my eye I saw two more medics carrying a stretcher toward the other ambulance. Lying on the stretcher was Dr. Burr.

The medic helped me in beside Carson.

"We're going to give you some oxygen," she said. "Do you have any pain anywhere?"

I shook my head. I still couldn't speak.

The medic fastened an oxygen mask like Carson's around my face. In a moment, I felt cool clear air in my nose and mouth. I gulped at it.

"We're just going to take you girls over to the hospital to check you out," the medic informed us. "You've been through a lot here tonight. We want to make sure you're okay."

She jumped inside with us and closed the double doors. The engine started, and I glanced over at Carson. Her face was smeared with soot and ash, and she looked pale. I could tell that she was as exhausted as I was.

Still, as she met my eyes, she managed a smile behind her oxygen mask. She lifted her hands and made a sign with them, starting with her two thumbs touching and her two index fingers touching. Bringing her hands in a circular motion away from her body, she brought them to a close again, this time with her two pinkies touching. I wasn't sure exactly what she meant, but I had a sense that she was probably feeling the same way I was: exhausted, but proud—and grateful.

I managed to flash her a thumbs-up in return. As the ambulance took off down the road, I breathed deeply and gazed around. My eyes came to rest on Carson's junior ranger badge, still pinned to her sweatshirt.

The edge of the plastic covering on the badge had melted from the heat of the fire, but the words printed across the bottom were still visible in the reflected swirling red light.

RANGER UNIT LEARNING EXTENSION

R.U.L.E., I thought, focusing on the largest letters on the badge. *The initials spell "rule,"* I realized suddenly. *I never noticed that before. I guess that makes us "Girls R.U.L.E."*

"Girls rule," I repeated to myself in a whisper. I managed a grin behind my mask. "I like the sound of that."

EIGHTEEN

I fell backward from the impact of a blow to my midsection and let out a gasp. Quickly, I rolled to the side and jumped to my feet. But he was headed straight for me.

Use the force of his attack to get him down, I reminded myself. *Work with his movement, not against it.*

Stepping forward, I shifted to the left to avoid his attack and locked my right leg behind my opponent's left knee. I caught him off guard and he lost his balance, tumbling to the floor. Lowering myself over him, I braced my knee against his chest and put my hand to his throat.

A moment later, I released him, and he stood up. We faced each other and bowed.

"Boy, I really thought I had you that time, Kayla," he said as we walked out of the studio and headed down the hall toward the changing rooms.

"You were close, Jeff," I told him. "Want to work out together again tomorrow?"

Jeff grinned. "It's the only way I'm ever going to make

purple belt." He headed toward the men's changing room. "See you tomorrow!"

"Okay, see you!" I replied.

I spotted my father down the hall, by the reception desk. He was dressed in his white karate suit, or *gi*, with his black belt wound around his waist. He was busy hanging something up on the wall in a frame.

"Hi, Dad," I said, walking over to him. "What are you doing?"

He smiled at me. "Take a look for yourself, honey. I framed the front page of the article from the *Echo*."

"Oh, Dad," I said. "You didn't have to hang it up!"

"I certainly did!" he objected. "How else was I going to make sure that every single person who stepped into this dojo knows that I'm the proudest father in the world?"

I laughed. "Hey, listen, did Mom drop off that package for me?" I asked.

"She sure did." He walked behind the reception desk and took out a small parcel, which he handed to me.

"Thanks," I said. I glanced up at the clock behind the desk. "I better run. The gang's expecting me."

"Kayla, before you go . . . ," my father began.

"Yes?"

He smiled. "Did I happen to mention how proud I am of you?"

I laughed. "I think so, Dad. But thanks again."

A little while later, Becca, Carson, Sophie, Alex, and I sat around a big table at the Cayenga Grill, munching on nachos and spinach pizza.

Cayenga Echo

OCTOBER 22, 1998   VOLUME 20, NO. 28   CAYENGA, CALIFORNIA

GIRLS' R.U.L.E. TO THE RESCUE

Five local girls save Cayenga Park from flames and more

OCTOBER 22: The five newest members of Cayenga Park's Ranger Unit Learning Extension are credited with saving countless trees and wildlife—and perhaps the entire park—from destruction by fire late Saturday night. The fire, which has been ruled "suspicious," broke out shortly before 11:00 P.M., park officials said today. The five girls, Kayla Adams, Becca Fisher, Alex Loomis-Drake, Carson McDonald, and Sophie Shultz, are all members of the recently created girls' division of the junior rangers. They were spending the night on Mesa del Oro, one of the park's highest mountains, as part of a survival trip

(continued on page 3)

"Researcher" Hid Secret Lab for Cruel Experiments, Park Officials Say

OCTOBER 22: The discovery yesterday of eighteen injured and sick raccoons at what was supposed to be a wildlife research center left park workers "shocked and saddened," according to supervising Ranger Abe Mayfield. Dr. Lyle Burr, who was supposedly conducting research at the center, was injured in a car accident near the scene of Saturday's fire and was taken to the hospital. Police are

(continued on page 5)

I gazed out the plate glass window at the view of the park. "Look," I said. "You can see a little patch of brown on Mesa del Oro where the fire was."

"The damage looks much worse on the other side," Alex said. "I can see it from the music room in our house."

"You have a music room?" Sophie said, obviously impressed. "That sounds great. What do you do there?"

Alex laughed. "Nothing, really. It's pretty much just a place to keep the piano. It's kind of silly, actually, since no one in our family even plays it."

"I wonder how long it will be before the mountain looks green again," Becca said wistfully.

"My mom said the rangers think it'll take a couple of years before things really start to grow back," Carson said.

"I can't believe someone would actually set a fire like that on purpose," Sophie said with disgust. "That Dr. Burr must have been completely crazy."

"That's for sure," I agreed. "Look at what he did to those poor raccoons!"

Sophie shivered. "I hate to think about it. I'll never forget the way they shrieked like that."

"I guess the one you heard in the woods earlier that day was caught in a trap or something," Alex said.

"And it must have been Dr. Burr who set the trap that Carson and I saw by the river the day of the test," Sophie added.

"Was he really catching all these animals just so he could give them rabies?" Becca asked. "Somehow it just doesn't make sense."

"Actually, my mom told me that when Dr. Burr first started out in the park, he was trying to *stop* the spread of rabies," Carson explained. "He did a really good job of it, too. But all those years of living alone in the woods must have gotten to him after a while, and he kind of lost sight of what he was supposed to be doing. Eventually, he started trapping raccoons and giving them the disease on purpose just so he could study it."

"Well, whatever he was doing, he was obviously out to make the five of us quit, or look bad, or both," I put in.

"They say he totally flipped when he heard that Ms. Rodriguez was thinking of investigating his research program to see if it could be cut to make room for the new girls' division," Alex said.

"Yeah, I suppose he was always allowed to do his so-called work on his own, and he didn't want to be investigated," Carson added. "And now we know why."

"I guess Dr. Burr figured he'd try to scare us out of the program. First he stole all our applications from the office so he could call our houses and pretend to be a ranger," Sophie said.

"Except for Carson," Alex put in. "He saw on her application that her mom was a ranger, so he knew he couldn't try that at her house."

"When he didn't scare the rest us off with that lie about an outbreak of rabies in the park, he knew he had to try something more drastic," Becca said.

"Right," Sophie said. "Like stealing our food."

"And that bit with the cap and the knife," Alex added.

"And don't forget the raccoon in my tent!" I put in.

"Not to mention starting a fire in our campsite and hoping it would be blamed on us," Carson said. She shook her head. "He was ready to do whatever it took to get us out of the park."

"Yeah, but now he's the one who's out," I said. I grinned at Becca and Alex. "It's karma, just like I told you about. What goes around comes back around to you."

"I hope they put him in jail for a long, long time," Sophie said.

Carson grinned. "I guess Dr. Burr didn't realize who he was up against."

"That's right!" Becca agreed. She grinned. "Nobody'll mess with the girls' division again, not after this!"

"Yeah, tell that to the boys!" Sophie said.

"You'd think they'd be grateful," I said, shaking my head. "After all, we pretty much saved their lives."

"That's not how Rick tells it," Sophie said. "According to him, they would have smelled the smoke and gotten off the mountain okay on their own." She rolled her eyes. "He and my brother even tried to say that they could have stopped the fire sooner than we did if *they'd* been on our side of the mountain."

Suddenly, I remembered something. "Hey, Carson, there's something I've been meaning to ask you," I said. "Remember when we were in the ambulance on our way to the hospital?"

Carson nodded. "Sure."

"What was that sign you gave me with your hands?" I asked. "Does it actually mean something?"

Carson repeated the sign, making a large O with her

thumbs and forefingers, separating her hands and moving them in a circular motion away from her body, then bringing them together again with pinkies touching.

"Yeah, that's it!" I said.

"It's American Sign Language," Carson explained. "I learned it when I was little." She smiled. "That's the sign for 'team.' Sitting there with that oxygen mask on my mouth, I couldn't really talk to you, Kayla, but I wanted to somehow say what I was feeling."

I smiled. "I think I got the message," I told her.

Sophie tried signing the word. "Is this right?" she asked Carson.

Carson nodded. "Perfect."

Alex smiled. "I like it. Team." She made the sign. "It can be like our own personal symbol."

"Hey, speaking of our own personal symbol, that reminds me," I said. I reached into my bag and pulled out the brown paper parcel. "Wait till you guys see these."

I unwrapped the package. Inside were several cloth patches.

"Here, look." I passed the patches around the table.

"These are incredible!" Sophie said, her face lighting up.

"Totally cool," Becca agreed.

"I love them!" Alex exclaimed.

"Kayla, where did you get these?" Carson wanted to know.

"My mom designed them for us and had them made up," I replied. "And I talked to Ranger Abe, and he says we can put them on all our park T-shirts, caps, and jackets."

I looked down at the patch in my hands with pride.

girls
R. U. L. E.

I grinned. "Now we're our own team for sure. From now on, the five of us aren't just the girls' division of the junior rangers. We're GIRLS R.U.L.E.!"

"Girls rule!" the others echoed enthusiastically.

ALL-NEW! ALL-EXCITING! ALL GIRL-FRIENDLY!
GRAND PRIZE: $500 WORTH OF CAMPING EQUIPMENT. 50 RUNNERS-UP: GIRLS R.U.L.E. T-SHIRTS.

No purchase necessary. For complete details see below. To enter the drawing, fill in the information below and return it to:

girls R.U.L.E.

375 Hudson Street, Dept. JH
New York, New York 10014

NAME_____

ADDRESS_____

CITY_____STATE_____

ZIP_____PHONE #_____

Mail this entry form or a plain 3" x 5" piece of paper postmarked no later than 12/31/98.

1. On an official entry form or a plain 3" x 5" piece of paper print or type your name, address, and telephone number and mail your entry to GIRLS R.U.L.E. SWEEPSTAKES, THE BERKLEY PUBLISHING GROUP, DEPT. JH, 375 Hudson Street, New York, New York 10014. No purchase necessary.

2. Entries must be postmarked no later than December 31, 1998. Not responsible for lost or misdirected mail. Enter as often as you wish, but each entry must be mailed separately.

3. The winner will be determined in a random drawing on January 8, 1999. The winner will be notified by mail.

4. This drawing is open to all U.S. and Canadian (excluding Quebec) residents age 13 and over. If a resident of Canada is selected in the drawing, he or she may be required to correctly answer a skill question to claim a prize. Void where prohibited by law. Employees (and their families) of Penguin Putnam Inc., Pearson, plc and their respective affiliates, retailers, distributors, advertising, promotion and production agencies are not eligible.

5. Taxes are the sole responsibility of the prize-winner. The name and likeness of the winner may be used for promotional purposes. The winner will be required to sign and return a statement of eligibility and liability/promotional release within 14 days of notification.

6. No substitution of the prize is permitted. The prize is non-transferable.

7. In the event there is an insufficient number of entries, the sponsor reserves the right not to award the prize.

8. For the name of the prize-winner, send a self-addressed, stamped envelope to GIRLS R.U.L.E. SWEEPSTAKES, Dept. JH, The Berkley Publishing Group, 375 Hudson Street, New York, NY 10014.

9. The Berkley Publishing Group and its affiliates, successors and assigns are not responsible for any claims or injuries of contestants in connection with the contest or prizes.